Cooke Concrete

Concrete Media, Incorporated
www.CookeConcrete.com
ISBN-13: 978-0692865620
ISBN-10: 0692865624

For Delia

1.

My roommate my freshman year was a skinny guy named Mike. He had a collection of hats and canes that he kept in our shared closet. Every once in a while I'd come home to him playing the trombone in our dorm room. We had different personalities but we got along well.

On our last night in the dorms, we got drunk together and Mike, a philosophy major, started asking questions at a depth that I generally try to avoid.

"What would you say is your major flaw?" he asked as he leaned back in his chair, teetering on the hind legs. The bay windows were open and the sounds of drunk coeds echoed in the street.

"It seems you have something in mind," I said as I sipped from the pint of vodka I had bought from a guy up the hall.

"Guilty," Mike said and smiled. "It's something I've been wanting to tell you all year. I really think you should know this," he said.

"It sounds like I should."

Mike laughed and then told me what I already knew. That I was not living up to my potential. That I could do more and if I didn't start to do more then it would come back to haunt me.

"Try or die," he said, nodding his head as he finished his diagnosis.

He turned to the window and screamed at the voices coming from outside: "Try or die!"

2.

On my first day home from college, I go to the park district to ask for my old job back. I put on a nice white shirt and a pair of khaki pants. Before leaving, I go out behind my parents' garage to have a cigarette. The day is so humid that the air seems more physical, more difficult to move through. Underneath my pants, beads of sweat trickle down my legs, tickling leg hairs on the path to my socks.

On my way to the offices, I walk past houses that grow larger as I get closer to the center of town. The sun reflects off everything and I curse myself for not having a pair of sunglasses.

It's a relief to arrive at the district offices and walk into the comparatively cool shadows of the utility garage behind the greenhouse. I walk through the garage, past a giant pile of mulch, and into the attached office.

Dave's on the phone. He smiles at me when I enter. He raises his index finger, gesturing that it will be a minute. He leans forward, the phone tucked between his shoulder and his neck. He fires off a string of 'uh-huh's and 'yeah's in the dull, professional voice that he reserves for higher-ups.

I look around the office. Cement floors, beige tiles on the walls, two filing cabinets standing side-by-side. Dave has hung several honorary plaques on the wall. As I breath, I taste the mulch in the air.

Dave finishes with a twangy 'alright' and claps the phone

into the cradle. He leans back in his chair and smiles. One of his front teeth is tinted brown.

"Look who it is," he coos, his southern accent returning.

I smile and nod. "It's me," I say.

"How's school?" he asks.

"It's alright. Not bad."

"Home for the summer or just visiting?"

"Home."

He leans forward.

"No summer school?" he asks.

"No," I say. "Not this summer."

"No internships?"

"No."

He nods. "Alright," he says. He seems disappointed that I am here. He wishes I had chosen to do something more productive with my summer interim.

"Actually," I say, trying to sound upbeat. "That's kind of why I stopped by. I was wondering if you might be looking for help this summer."

Dave leans back and scratches his beard. He looks over my shoulder into the corner of the room as if something there might give him the answer.

"Well," he says and then pauses. "I might be able to come up with something. They've really tightened their belts around here. I've already got one guy working for me. I might be able to get you something part-time."

"That would be great," I say.

"I could maybe patch together a couple different types of hours for you. Get you some additional work in the offices. Something that might build your resume."

"That would be great," I say again, even though I would rather forego the office work.

I have nothing else to do for the day so I walk over to the library. The library is an impressive structure whose shiny white coating lends it a futuristic feel. The sliding doors of the library automatically part as I approach and I'm enveloped by chilled air. There is an old woman sitting behind a welcome desk in the center of the foyer.

"Hello," she says and smiles.

"Hi," I say.

The library is almost empty. The heat has kept people home. There are several people reading books in the cafe and there's a cute girl about my age behind the checkout desk.

I walk up the slate steps to the second floor. I go to the stacks and search for something to read. The selection seems mundane compared to the books I found in the vast window-less stacks of the library at school. The nicer a library looks, the less gravitas it seems to have. I pick a slim book by an author I've read before.

I go back down to the first floor and stand in line at the checkout desk behind a mother and her two children. I look around as I wait and I notice a man sitting in the cafe, stooped over a notebook. He is writing with intensity, the little wisps of hair at the front of his balding head wave with the movements of his pen.

The balding man looks up for a moment and I see that it's not actually an old man. It's Adam Pazsitsky. His hairline has dramatically receded since I last saw him but his face still has an ageless cherubic quality.

Adam sees me and nods. He doesn't smile; there is a blank-ness to his face now. I smile and nod back.

"Next," says the librarian. I turn from Adam and hand my book to the librarian. She turns the book sideways.

"Short," she says. "My kind of book."

She has a protruding snaggletooth on one side of her mouth like she's half a vampire.

"You don't like to read?" I ask.

"I like to read," she says. "I just like short books."

I nod at her response to indicate that it's alright with me.

3.

At the dinner table, my parents are pleasant and respectful. It's mostly statements on their parts, few questions. They discuss changes on the block. New neighbors, new construction. They are careful not to bring up my performance at college. Their dance around the subject makes it more present, not less. They outline its shape through avoidance.

I go upstairs after dinner and lay on my bed with the windows open. I read the book that I got from the library, stopping from time to time to listen to the whirring insects outside and look around my room.

After I left for college, my parents converted my bedroom into a combination guest room and office. They've added a desk and an old empty dresser. Next to the desk, my dad built a tall wooden shelf that's divided into tiny compartments which he uses to organize a variety of things, mostly old electronics. Each compartment is neatly labeled with a small tag to identify the contents. The shelves have a vaguely taxonomic feel and my eyes are continually drawn to it.

While I'm reading, my cell phone rings. I look at the display and see that it's Lindsay. I stand up from my bed and look at the phone. After three rings of consideration, I flip it open.

"Hey," I say.

"You answered," says Lindsay.

I look down at my feet. "Did I?" I ask.

"How's it going?" she asks.

"Not bad."

I imagine Lindsay is at home, probably on her back porch. She never used to call me in front of her parents.

"Are you home for the summer?" she asks.

"Maybe," I say, purposefully vague. "Are you?"

She groans.

"I am," she says.

"You're not taking summer classes?"

"No, I'm interning downtown at a consulting firm."

"Oh," I say. "Sounds impressive."

She groans again but it sounds disingenuous.

"It's not. It's grunt work and it's boring and it takes me an hour to get there each day."

"Huh," I say.

"What about you?" she asks.

"I don't know yet. I think I might be getting my job at the park district back."

"Oh," she says carefully. "That's cool."

"Yeah. Not bad."

"So you are in town."

"I might be."

She laughs but I sense my avoidance is wearing thin.

"Well, if you were in town, would you want to do something some time?"

"Like what?"

"I don't know," she says. "Maybe go for a run?"

"I would probably do that," I say.

We agree to meet the next afternoon. Running seems like an ideal activity to do with Lindsay. There would be less talking and fewer questions about my first year at school. Plus, I'm a pretty good runner and although Lindsay may have a more impressive summer job than me, I'm confident that I can still run faster than her.

The next day, I arrive at the gazebo before Lindsay and I stretch out on the grass while I wait. I notice how doughy my legs have become. I hear laughing as I stretch and I turn to see

Lindsay smiling as she walks towards me. She's become more beautiful over the past year. Her skin is bronzed and she's done something to her hair that gives it a golden tint.

"Look who it is," she says.

"It is I," I say, standing. We hug and step back from one another.

"Look at you," she says.

"Look at you," I say.

After stretching, we start running and I quickly realize that I've lost whatever physical edge that I once had over Lindsay. It's clear that she has been exercising during the school year while I haven't broken a sweat since last summer.

By the time we reach the bridge over the expressway, I'm struggling to hold pace.

"Are you okay" asks Lindsay, chuckling.

"I'm fine," I rasp.

"Do you want to stop?" she asks.

"No," I say. "Let's keep going."

After we finish our run, Lindsay and I sit down in the field behind the gazebo. I'm drenched in sweat. Lindsay glows; only the hair around her temples is damp. It sticks to the side of her face in dark curlicues. I lay back on the grass and look up at the sky. I watch clouds move. Strands of grass tickle my legs.

"Nice day," I say.

Lindsay nods.

I sit up and pull a heel up into my crotch and reach towards my other leg. A hurdler's stretch. I savor the sting.

"Let me ask you something," I say as I cling to my far foot. "When did you start running?"

"I don't know," says Lindsay.

"Does your mom run?"

"No."

"Does your dad?"

"No. Why?"

"I don't know. I'm just curious how you started."

She's quiet for a moment.

"I was a good runner in gym class," she says. "And I liked it, so I started doing cross country in junior high and I did well in the meets."

"Did you win medals?"

She smiles.

"I won a lot of them. Mostly second place medals. Stephanie Kilner always took first."

"I remember her. She had really dry skin. She maybe had a condition."

Lindsay smiles.

"She was fast. And nice."

"Did it make you mad?"

Lindsay considers for a moment.

"Not really. I wanted to come in first and I did once or twice when Stephanie missed a meet. I was satisfied with my performance."

"You weren't mad that you didn't come in first more often?"

"No. I wanted it but I wasn't mad that I didn't get it."

"Okay."

Lindsay pauses and then laughs.

"Why?"

"No reason," I say. "Just curious."

"Okay."

She laughs again.

"I think I would be mad if I kept getting second," I say.

Lindsay shrugs. "I don't know."

I think I believe Lindsay when she says she's okay with second place.

We continue to stretch. I stick my legs out straight in front of me and pull my chest down towards them. I feel pain in my hips and behind my knees. It feels incredible. I don't know why I didn't work out at college.

"I met a guy at a party who said he didn't stretch before lifting weights and he snapped his pectoral tendon."

"No!" cries Lindsay.

"He said there was a loud pop and the tendon coiled up into the muscle like that—"

I spin my index fingers around one another.

"Did the weight fall on him?"

"I don't know," I say. "I assume he had a spotter."

Lindsay is quiet for a moment.

"What are you doing tonight?"

"I don't know," I say. "Why?"

"Do you want to come to my brother's party?"

"What's it for?"

"Graduation and birthday."

"Will your parents be there?"

Lindsay laughs.

"Of course they will."

"I don't know if I want to see your dad."

Lindsay shakes her head.

"Would you get over that?" Lindsay asks. I hear frustration in her voice.

I hate Lindsay's dad. There are only a few people I've ever fantasized violence towards and Lindsay's dad is one of them. I hate Mr. Cooke because he condescends to me. I've tried to explain this to Lindsay but she says I'm making it up. I'm not making it up.

I'll give an example about the condescension. Last summer, I was at the Cooke's for dinner and they were talking about skiing and I was just listening because I've never been skiing before. Mrs. Cooke saw I was being quiet and tried to include me in the conversation by asking if I had ever been skiing. I said no, I had never been skiing but, nonetheless, I had the feeling I would be good at it.

I said this in sort of a playful tone but it also happens to be true. It's hard to explain but I thought I would make a good skier from the times when I saw other people skiing. Anyway, when I said what I did about skiing the table got kind of quiet as if I had just said something stupid. Of course, I had said something stupid but I had said it intentionally and in a joking tone.

After a disheartening silence, Mr. Cooke took a sip of water and asked how I could tell I would be good at a sport if I had never done it.

"I don't know," I said. "I just have a feeling about it."

I chuckled. "I mean, I'm sort of kidding," I explained.

I looked over at Lindsay who forced a smile and looked down at her plate. That really upset me. She could have at least joked along with me or made a joke about how bad my joke was. It was an uncomfortable moment that left me feeling inferior and stupid.

After we finished dinner, Lindsay and I went out to the back porch. Lindsay laid down on a deck chair and I stood across from her with my hands in my pockets.

"Ugh," she said, and closed her eyes. "My stomach hurts."

I didn't respond, hoping she would notice my silence. She either didn't notice the silence or didn't want to comment on it. She just laid there with her head back and her eyes closed. After a few minutes, I walked away and made my way home without saying goodbye.

4.

After running with Lindsay, I go home and shower. The heat of the water feels earned. I taste salt as the hot water washes down my forehead and into my mouth. I think about the night. I consider what I would do if I went out. I don't have many options. None of my other friends are home for the summer.

I get a text from Lindsay. "Are you coming?" it asks.

"Maybe," I text back.

I go upstairs to my room and dress for the party. I put on a white polo and a pair of khakis. People will be dressed nice at this thing. I've gone to Cooke family parties before and there are always loafers and dress pants.

I glance at myself in the mirror. I look like a blue blood. I search around for something to set me apart and I find an old necklace in my dresser that I made when I was at camp in junior high. The necklace is made of pink and yellow clay beads strung together with a leather string. It's hideous.

When I get to the Cooke's, I follow the lights and voices up the long drive into the backyard. People are walking around and talking. I see a series of faces that I don't recognize. Relatives of Lindsay, all well-dressed and a little paunchy. These people look so relaxed and pleasant; they wear their success like comfortable shoes.

As I come up the steps to the back porch, I look out into the backyard. It is deep and dark and seems to go on forever.

I see Lindsay talking to someone over by the railing. She sees me, smiles, walks over.

"Hey," I say.

"Hey," she says and I see her eyes linger on my necklace for a moment.

"What?" I ask.

"What?" she says and laughs. "Nothing."

"You don't like my necklace?" I ask.

"No!" she says, her eyes going wide. "It's fine. What is your problem?"

"Nothing," I say.

"Je-*sus*," she says and laughs.

"I'm going to get something to drink. There are drinks?"

"Yeah," she says. "In the kitchen."

On my way to the kitchen, I see Mitch, Lindsay's brother. He's with a group of kids who are all gathered around a piano. They're not playing the piano; they're just talking and laughing. Mitch stands a little aside from the group, his hands in his pockets and his shoulders pulled back. I like Mitch. He's an awkward and chubby kid who always seems quietly befuddled at social events.

I nudge him with my elbow as I walk past.

"So this is all because you graduated junior high?" I ask. He smiles.

"Yeah," he says.

"You should be very proud," I say with mock seriousness.

"It's also my birthday."

"Oh," I say. "Lindsay didn't tell me that. I would have brought a gift."

He shrugs.

"I don't care."

"That's good," I say and wink at him.

I continue into the kitchen. There are a few people gathered there, talking and laughing. The counter is laid out with alcohol and mixers. I fill a clear plastic cup with ice and Coke.

No one seems to be watching so I pick up a bottle of Maker's Mark and try to splash a little into my drink. I misestimate and pour about two shots worth into the cup.

"Damn," I mutter and several people look towards me.

I walk around the party for a while, smiling at people and munching on an assortment of vegetables that I get from the spread on the dining room table. The alcohol gives me a buzz which makes the party warm and pleasant. I look for Lindsay in each room but I don't see her. I don't know anyone so I don't say anything. Instead, I pretend to look at photos and paintings on the walls while eavesdropping on conversations.

After a while, I make my way out onto the back porch again and look out into the yard. I squint to see if I can make out the back. I see no end to it and I get the idea that I want to walk all the way to the back. I start down the porch steps.

I notice a group of men on the driveway. They wear dress pants and boldly-colored silk shirts. I immediately spot Mr. Cooke's distinctive white hair at the center of the group. He smiles as he listens to these men, his head is tipped downward in a way that gives him a leer. These men are all taller and louder than him, but their loudness seems to be an effort to earn his appreciation. Mr. Cooke speaks less but is at the center of the conversation. When he does speak, his mouth moves with careful precision, laying down final judgements. He has a twinkle of self-satisfaction in his eyes as the men laugh at his comments.

For a moment, I imagine popping him in the nose with the top of a bat and I grit my teeth with delight at the thought of his nose splintering under the metal.

As I pass, I call out to him.

"Mr. Cooke," I say.

All of the men turn and look. Mr. Cooke stares at me. He doesn't respond, he just waits for me to say something. I can't tell if he recognizes me.

"Nice shirt," I say and I make an okay sign with my hand.

I stumble a little as I turn and walk into the darkness of the backyard.

Behind me, I hear him say something to the group. All the men burst into laughter.

I don't feel like going home after I leave the Cookes so I drive around, looking at houses and enjoying the night. I find myself over by the quarry and I decide to drive down the dark street that bisects the quarry into two halves.

The quarry was once owned by Lindsay's family. Lindsay's great grandfather started it and then expanded the company. He built a cement processing plant and then bought a fleet of cement trucks and most of the sidewalks in town were laid by Cooke Concrete. The company name is stamped into the sidewalks to prove it. I used to point out the faded stamps to Lindsay every time we saw one just to watch her face grow red with embarrassment. About five years ago, the quarry stopped being mined and the Cookes sold it to the city for flood overflow.

My tires make a hollow twin thump as I come over the tracks and dip down into the street that cuts through the quarry. There aren't any lights or sidewalks. It's just a darkened strip of cement that runs across a giant gorge. On a whim, I flip off my headlights, press down on the accelerator, and speed into the darkness.

The night is cloudless and the moonlight casts everything ahead of me in a flat grey light. My windows are rolled down and there's a wild rumble of wind in my ears. A black blur of trees whiz by my periphery.

Out the passenger window, I notice a white bird perched on the metal guardrail that runs alongside the road. I crane my head forward to get a better look. I realize that it's not a bird but a shoe resting on the rail, toes pointed skyward.

I brake and pull over. I twist around in my seat. Through the back window, I can see the shoe from the side. It's red in the brake lights.

I open the car door and get out. I watch the leg to see if it moves.

"Hello?" I ask.

The leg remains still. The only sound I hear are chirping crickets.

I reach into the car and turn on the emergency lights. I pull back out of the car and walk towards the leg in the strobe of the hazards.

When I arrive at the leg, I stand in front of it and look down into the thicket. I can't see anything in there. Not a body, not a partner leg. Just thick weeds.

"Hello?" I say again.

I put my hand on the rubber sole of the shoe and shake it.

"Are you alright?" I ask.

There is no response.

I notice a small patch of skin between the sock and the cuff of the jeans. I put my fingers on the skin and press down. The skin is warm and I feel a coiled strand of leg hair under my fingertip.

The leg remains still.

"Hey," I say again.

No response.

I step over the guardrail. I lean forward and reach my arms into the weeds. I push them apart and look into the dark undergrowth for the body. The roots of the weeds bend into obscurity.

I grab more weeds and push them to the side.

This time, the weeds part to reveal the body in the grass. It is crumpled up into a strange pose like a newborn baby locked in a flail.

My first impulse is to jump away from it. I don't though.

"Hey!" I yell at it.

I don't think these words before I say them. There are too many thoughts in my head at once. I simply act on those which arrive first.

In the moonlight, I run my eyes over the body to see what has happened. The face is not visible; it's turned sideways into the weeds. The clothes are dark. The other leg is bent underneath him.

My eyes land on a collection of tiny glowing points at the center of his chest. For a moment, I don't believe I see these luminous pinpoints until I realize I am looking at a glow-in-the-dark shirt of the constellations.

I bend over the body to touch it but I stop myself. I move back from the body and stand for a moment. I then break into action and hurdle the guardrail.

In my car, it is as if I'm driving for the first time. Everything moves too slow. I put the car in drive and step on the accelerator. My headlights are still off—which I don't realize—and I struggle to see the road ahead of me.

I clear the dark stretch of road and drive into a lit street. I park my car in front of the first home I see: A boxy house with a screened-in front porch. I hurry along the front walk, up the front stairs, and pull on the porch door handle but it won't open.

"Come on," I hiss.

I pound my first on the edge of the screen door several times. I press a doorbell next to the mailbox, causing a pleasant chime inside. A series of lights finally illuminate and I hear voices and footsteps approaching.

The drapes of the porch window pull back. A woman's face looks out at me. I smile and put my hand up to wave. She stares at me longer than I anticipate and I stare back at her. I point towards the quarry.

"There was someone hit by a car," I say, exaggerating the words so she can hear me.

"Hit—by—a—car," I say again.

The drapes drop and I hear muffled talk behind the door. There is a click as the door is unlocked and the woman looks out at me from the narrow opening, across the chasm of the screened-in porch.

"What?" she says. I look at her pinched face.

"There was someone hit by a car," I say. "Over by the quarry. He's unconscious. Will you call for an ambulance? I don't have my phone with me."

The woman looks at me for a moment and then nods.

"Okay," she says. She shuts the door and I hear the deadbolt snap.

I stand in the street for several minutes wondering whether the woman has actually called an ambulance. I finally hear a siren in the distance. The woman walks out onto her front porch.

"They're coming," she says.

"Thanks," I say.

I get in my car and drive back towards the body. I park across from it and put my hazards on again so the ambulance will know where to come.

I listen to the wail of the siren gradually growing louder and look at the leg from across the street. I walk over to the body and stand next to the shoe. It feels strange just standing next to a body. It occurs to me that I could be standing next to a dead person which would be a first for me.

About ten feet away, I notice a bike wheel sticking out of the grass like a shark fin. I walk over to it and look at the bike laying bent up in the grass. It's an old ten speed the color of rust.

When the ambulance and police arrive, I point out the body to the paramedics. The police officer leads me back across the street and has me explain how I found the body. I tell him the story but leave out the part about driving without my lights off. My attention is divided between the questions the officer asks me and the paramedics. I watch them as they step into the weeds and move the body onto a stretcher. As one of the paramedics steps back over the guardrail, the stretcher angles towards me and I see the the serious face and balding head of Adam Pazsitsky.

"Oh," I say.

"What?" asks the policeman, turning to look at the medics.

"I know him," I say.

5.

Dave calls and tells me he can give me my job back but only part-time. He wasn't able to get me any of the 're-sume-building' work in the offices. I'm relieved but try to sound disappointed. I prefer to work outdoors even if the district offices would fetch me more paid hours.

My days at work are spent riding from garden to garden with a squat, red-headed man named John. John is in his mid-fifties; a change from previous summers when I worked with high school students.

John had previously worked as a gravedigger at a local cemetery. I don't ask John how he lost his job but it becomes clear that John would be the first to go at any enterprise. He is an expert time-waster, frequently making stops for food or cigarettes while on the clock. Sometimes he won't work for the entire day; when we're at the gardens, he'll lean against the truck and smoke.

"I'm sorry, man," he'll explain. "I just can't today."

At first, I find John's incredible lack of ambition amusing but it irritates me after a while. I'm not working all that hard either. I stand around and water plants or pull a few weeds from the flowerbeds. Still, there is something insulting about an equal watching you work.

I keep my occasional flashes of anger at John under wraps and take consolation that John is, at the very least, a fasci-nating individual to watch function. He frequently describes his struggles with bipolarity. "I ever tell you about the time I painted my entire house in a weekend?" he'll ask and then launch into a story detailing a frantic dash to complete a labor-intensive task within a narrow window of time. John tries to make his stories amusing but, more often than not, they're depressing and that's why I like them.

After several weeks, I start to notice these peaks and valleys in John's moods. Some days, John is followed into work by a dark aura. We'll drive around all day in stony silence with the radio off. Other days, John works at a pace so furiously manic that it borders on destructive. He'll blare grating pop music on the radio and talk non-stop. At the gardens, he'll start to rip out weeds but move with such reckless speed that he'll rip out numerous healthy flowers as well. Some flowers he tamps back into place with the heel of his palm, others he lobs into the back of the truck with the rest of the weeds. I ask him about this one day, pointing my trowel at the colorful flowers in the bed of the truck. He looks at them for a moment then flashes a yellow smile and says: "I don't discriminate." This makes me laugh.

John talks a lot about his last job at the cemetery. He describes tricks he played on a co-worker named Samuel. When John says Samuel's name, he sneers a little, as if the name itself carries a rotten flavor. "With a name like Samuel," says John. "You know he's a worm."

"I've got a tape around somewhere of the guys at work teasing him," he tells me one day. "It's the funniest thing you'll ever see."

I tell John I'd like to see the tape even though it seems wrong to watch it. I feel guilty both for treating John's peculiar personality as a form of amusement and for indulging the pleasure John takes in teasing a grown man.

"I'll see if I can find it," says John. "I've got it around somewhere."

I park in the hospital lot and walk through the hot breath of the blacktop towards the sliding doors. I tell the nurse at reception that I'm here to see Adam Pazsitsky.

"Third floor," she says, and points me towards the elevators.

The elevator is spacious and slow-moving and hums in a way that reminds me of an x-ray machine. There's something mechanized about hospitals that gives me the creeps.

When I enter Adam's room, he's lying in bed with a large white bandage covering one side of his forehead like some sort of weird hat. He's looking at a wall-mounted television, watching a nature show with the volume muted and the subtitles on. A nature show seems about right for Adam.

Mrs. Pazsitsky sits in a chair across from him. She's reading a book. She looks like a pile of dirty laundry. I try to imagine the job she works and I can only picture something in a non-descript office or maybe a hall monitor. She's wearing brown polyester pants and a dirty floral print sweater. Her glasses are thick and tinted brown, her hair is frizzy and curly. She has an impressive wattle under her neck. She smiles wanly when I enter.

"Hi," I say.

"Hello," says Mrs. Pazsitsky. She has something in her throat so the greeting comes out as a rasp.

Adam looks over at me and clicks off the TV.

"I'm Vince Ford," I say to Mrs. Pazsitsky.

Mrs. Pazsitsky grunts as she stands. This seems to take more effort than it should for a woman her age.

"I remember you," she says though I don't remember ever having met her. She still hasn't cleared her throat and her rasping voice grates on me.

"Hey Adam," I say. He looks so thin.

"Hey," he mumbles, his mouth small and tensed. He doesn't look at me. He looks at my shirt.

"How are you feeling?" I ask.

"I'm alright," he says and then pauses. "It doesn't hurt."

"We want to thank you," says Mrs. Pazsitsky.

Adam nods.

"Yes. Thank you," he says.

"I didn't do much," I say. "I'm glad I saw your shoe."

Adam makes eye contact with me for the first time.

"That's how you spotted me?" he asks. "My shoes?"

"Yeah," I say. "One of your feet was up on the guardrail."

It's odd looking at Adam with the large bandage across his head. It makes him somehow distant and difficult to read. There is a lull in the conversation and we all try to think of something to say. I don't know Adam well enough to go further with the conversation. I don't want to ask too many details about the accident but I don't know what else to say.

"Do you remember it?" I finally ask. It's the one question I actually want to know the answer to.

Adam looks out the window at the parking lot, at rows of shimmering windshields. He squints at the light.

"No," he mumbles. "I don't."

6.

In the fifth grade, I watched Adam walk away from a fight and into a stranger's house. The fight was with Pat Milchner, an insecure rich kid who had become aware of his own middling abilities. Pat was forever grasping at opportunities to prove himself a dominant leader.

In class, I heard about Pat's plan to fight Adam. My young conscience tried to resist the temptation to watch the fight but I wound up running to see it. I joined the pack of wide-eyed kids who had gathered on the front lawn of a white brick mansion.

When I arrived, Pat had pushed Adam off the sidewalk and onto the lawn. Adam kept trying to walk away.

"I don't want to fight," he muttered.

Pat clenched his teeth and swung at Adam's head. The punches looked soft until one caught Adam on the temple. He stumbled sideways and fell. His backpack flung forward and hit him in the back of the head with an audible clunk.

Pat leapt on Adam's back and pummeled the sides of his head. Pat twisted at the hips as he swung each fist. Adam pushed upwards, rising against the weight of Pat.

As Pat fell backwards, he grabbed onto Adam's backpack and yanked it towards him. Adam let his body go slack and threw his arms forward. He slipped out of both his shirt and his backpack. Lacking the counterweight of Adam, Pat fell back. The sleeves of the now Adam-less shirt hung through the shoulder straps.

Adam got his balance. His back was towards us. We all stood there and looked at his skinny arms. A fine white hair coated his shoulders.

"Hey!" Pat called out to Adam.

Adam didn't respond. He just wobbled a little and then walked. We watched him. He walked across the lawn towards the house. He opened the front door of the house and went inside.

Pat's rage peaked when Adam closed the door. He ripped open the backpack and threw the books across the lawn. The group dissipated.

Later that night, I felt guilty for watching the fight. I thought about looking Adam up in the school directory to call and apologize for not helping him but I decided against it.

7.

The sun is just starting to dip below the horizon as I pull into the Cooke's driveway. The light of the sunset turns the world a dark orange. Mr. Cooke is out in the yard, on his knees, stooped towards his garden. That's one of the things I've never understood about Mr. Cooke. He likes to garden. He spends a lot of time on it. I told Lindsay one time that gardening didn't fit her father's personality. She said it fits if you know him.

When I pull into the driveway, Mr. Cooke sits up and turns to look at my car. Lindsay walks down the driveway. Mr. Cooke says something to her. She looks at him and says something back as she continues towards my car.

"Hey," she says as she opens the passenger side door and gets in.

"Hey," I say.

She shuts the door.

"What did your dad say to you?" I ask.

She smiles.

"None of your business."

"I bet it was about me," I say.

We drive down the highway and exit onto a frontage road that runs alongside the highway. We drive past a Walmart to a small amusement park that is lit from above by panels of flood lights. The amusement park has a go-kart track, batting cages, and a mini-golf course. I like this place. Someone took an unused parking lot and turned it into something.

We collect our clubs at the Tiki hut next to the course and stop at the first hole. It's a flat green with no obstacles.

"You want to go first?" I ask Lindsay.

"Sure," she says.

Lindsay sets her ball down on a hole punched into the black rubber mat. She slings her purse behind her hip and leans over the ball. Lindsay is an athletic person and I can see the singular focus of an athlete as she lines up her shot.

She hits the ball forward. It rolls along the green and drops in the hole.

She turns her head towards me and smiles.

"I'm the best," she says and laughs.

"We'll see," I say as I place my ball on the mat.

I take my shot. The golf ball looks like it's on a good path but it catches some invisible dip in the green and snakes to the left of the hole. Lindsay laughs, triumphant.

"It's the club," I say. "Let's switch."

"No," says Lindsay, clutching the club to her chest. "I like my club."

The second hole is built around a miniature windmill and the ball has to be hit through a slot at the base of the windmill into the hole on the other side. This has to be done without being blocked by the windmill blades which slowly sweep past the slot.

Lindsay steps up to the rubber mat.

"Do you play mini-golf a lot?" I ask.

"I play real golf with my dad."

"Oh," I say. "*Real* golf."

Lindsay hits the ball. It rolls between the blades, through the slot, and drops into the hole on the other side with a tinny clink.

"How is that possible?" I ask.

Lindsay beams at me.

I put my ball down on the black mat and line up again. I

take my time lining up the putter.

I can feel that the shot is bad as soon as I take it. The ball hits the side of the slot and rolls back towards me. I try to stop the ball with the head of my club but I miss. I chase after the ball as it rolls across the pebbly concrete and drops into a mini pond. I look into the water. I expect the ball will float but it doesn't. Or if it does, I don't see it. I turn to Lindsay who is laughing.

"I lost my ball," I say.

I go back to the Tiki hut and explain to the kid behind the counter that my ball didn't float.

"They always float," he says.

Lindsay sits in quiet contentment during the car ride home. The self-satisfaction comes off her like heat.

"Congratulations," I say.

"You got that last one," she says.

"I did. That's true."

I can see Lindsay smile as she looks out her window.

I turn my car into Lindsay's driveway. The headlights roll across the neighbor's lawn and swing over to the garage. The beams fall on Mr. Cooke at the top of the drive. He stands in front of the garage with his hands in his pockets. He looks like a ghost up there, his white hair glowing in the light.

"There's your dad," I say.

Mr. Cooke looks up. The headlights reflect off his glasses. His eyes stay on us for a moment and I feel like he's looking straight at me even though he probably can't see me in the car. After a moment, he tilts his head back towards the driveway and carefully slides the toe of his shoe across the ground.

I squint my eyes.

"What's he doing?" I ask.

"He's looking at the cracks in the driveway."

"Why?" I ask.

"Would you be interested in sealing our driveway?"

I look at her.

"Huh?"

"My dad wants someone to re-seal it. He wants me to ask my friends."

I recall goading Mr. Cooke about his shirt at the party.

"Does he remember who I am?"

"Of course," she says.

"He can't get a professional to do it?"

"He says they overcharge. He'll pay you."

"Your dad is one of the Cookes of Cooke Concrete."

"They sold that years ago."

"He can't afford to pay someone?"

"You don't have to do it."

I can tell from the expression on Lindsay's face that she doesn't think there's anything odd about the question. She's not asking to upset me. I try to transcend the frustration that her question stirs in me. Maybe Lindsay is right; maybe her father's condescension is in my head.

I take a breath.

"Sure," I say, sighing out the word. "Why not."

8

When I go downstairs to eat breakfast, I find the house empty. It's a weekend and I've slept late into the morning. At college, all of my second semester classes were in the afternoon and my body falls back into the schedule with ease.

I pour myself a bowl of cereal and open the refrigerator. The gallon of milk is almost empty. I'm about to curse whoever left it in the refrigerator until I remember that it was me.

I leave the bowl of dry cereal on the counter and go out to the garage. I wheel out my mom's bike. I could take my dad's bike but my mom's has one of those gelatin seats that are really comfortable.

I ride down the block and cross over the railroad tracks that follow the running path down towards the White Hen. There are trees along either side of the path, so it's shaded and pleasant. I ride until the path meets Maple where I turn and pedal over to the White Hen. I buy the milk then head back up Maple. I ride with one hand on the handlebar. The other hand, slung to the side, holds the plastic bag with the milk in it.

For variety, I take a different route home. I go past the businesses on Maple and then turn down a residential street that takes me past condos, an apartment complex, over the tracks, and back into houses. As I ride, my mind turns to these two religious kids who lived on the same floor as me at school. I don't know why I think of them. Their names were Tim and Landon and they always seemed so content. They'd walk around the dorm, always with a smile on their faces, always looking so healthy. I'm still thinking about these kids as I turn down the block that's several over from my house. Going down this block is a roundabout route for me to take but I'm enjoying the time spent reflecting on things and it's a nice day and I want to keep riding.

I look at the houses I'm passing and my eyes land on a dilapidated white house that is so mediocre it's almost invisible. The lawn and the bushes are overgrown and the drooping gutter is filled with ancient leaves. A person's eyes would normally pass over this house and the only reason mine don't is that it's Adam's house.

I notice Mrs. Pazsitsky shuffling backwards down the driveway, dragging a sizable tree limb behind her. Her back is towards me, her shiny polyester shirt stretched so tight that the edges of her bras strap and the contour of her wide back are visible underneath.

I turn my bike up onto the sidewalk and flick down the kickstand. I set down the gallon of milk next to my bike.

"Here," I call out to Mrs. Pazsitsky. "I'll get that."

Mrs. Pazsitsky lets go of the tree limb and looks over at me. Her face is red from exertion. Beads of sweat collect on her brow. She shakes her head a little as if she doesn't want to accept my offer but then whispers 'okay' as she catches her breath and steps away from the tree branch. She grimaces as she rotates one of her shoulders and massages it with her opposite hand.

"Your shoulder alright?" I ask.

"Fine," she mutters.

The tree limb is very large, maybe the size of a small car. Its leaves are still green which means it hasn't fallen long ago and there hasn't been a storm in a while so it probably came from a sick tree. I grip the branch by the center limb. It's as thick as my calf. I lean backwards and it slides towards me.

"This is heavy," I say. "Shouldn't Adam be doing this for

you?"

I smile at her to let her know I'm kidding. She looks at the tree branch, not at me. She has a scowl on her face and I can't tell if it's from my question or the pain in her shoulder.

"I don't know where he is," she mumbles.

The branch makes a loud swishing sound as I tug it across the asphalt drive.

"He's not home today?" I ask.

"No," she says and hesitates. "I haven't seen him since the night before last."

"Huh," I say.

I stop asking questions and pull the branch across the lawn, grunting as I go. The grass on the lawn is thick and over-grown, difficult to get the branch across. Mrs. Pazsitsky follows a few feet behind, staring into the branch, never looking at me.

I stop at the curb. "Is this good here?" I ask between breathes.

"That's fine," she says.

I brush off my hands on my pants.

"So you haven't seen Adam for a few days?"

"No," she mumbles, stepping backward up the drive. I get the feeling she wants to avoid a conversation but doesn't want to be rude to someone who has just helped her.

"I'm sure he'll turn up," she adds as she turns away from me and walks up the driveway.

I look at the tree branch.

"The garbagemen take tree branches?" I call out to her.

She flaps her hand at her side as if shooing me away.

"Someone will take it," she says over her shoulder.

I turn the interaction over in my head as I ride home. It doesn't seem normal for someone like Adam to unexpectedly leave home for a few days. I wonder if maybe the head injury from the accident has affected his behavior. I feel bad about being suspicious of someone who is so pathetic and lonely but there was something unsettling about Mrs. Pazsitsky.

My parent's car is parked in the driveway when I return home. I put the bike back in the garage and walk up the back stairs. I stop at the back door and look in through the glass. The plastic handle of the milk is cool and wet in my hands.

Inside, I see my parents talking with my older brother Dennis and someone else. A young woman around whom Dennis has his arm. I forgot that Dennis was arriving today for a visit. The young lady is about a head shorter than Dennis. She has pretty eyes but her nose seems too big for her face and she hasn't given much consideration to her looks.

Dennis is saying something to my parents and they're leaning towards him. They nod their heads and listen close. I've always been amazed by Dennis's self-assuredness. He's able to talk about anything with competency.

I open the back door and everyone looks at me.

"Look who it is," says my mom, referring to Dennis.

"Hey," I say. "Welcome home."

"Thanks," says Dennis, smiling. I can see him instantly processing me, gathering information. He takes his arm from around his girlfriend and steps towards me. We hug. He places his hands flat on my back and I feel the warmth of his palms through my tee-shirt.

"It's good to see you," he says.

"Likewise," I say.

He steps out of the hug. "This is Pam," he says. Pam steps forward and smiles at me.

"Pam, this is my brother, Vince."

"Nice to meet you," says Pam as she goes in to hug.

"You too," I say.

At dinner, we ask Dennis and Pam a string of questions and they answer in tandem, completing one another's sentences as if they are the same person which, somehow, they seem to be. They're enrolled in the same program at MIT. They're interested in the same subjects. They have the same way about them: confident but not arrogant. There is no good reason to dislike either of them despite their unfair intellectual gifts.

"What projects are you working on at school?" my dad asks Pam after he finishes questioning Dennis.

Pam nods her head and swallows her food.

"I'm studying a method that would allow algae to be used as an alternate fuel source. It's not currently viable but we hope that it will be one day."

"Saving the world," I say.

Pam looks at me and smiles. "Hoping to make it better."

After my parents question Pam for a while, Pam starts asking questions of me and I can see in the way Dennis readjusts his posture that he's concerned she's going to ask a question that might offend me. I love Dennis but his need to keep things even keel can sometimes be frustrating. Fortunately, Pam asks questions out of good-natured curiosity.

"How do you like college, Vince?"

"I like it," I say.

"Maybe a little too much," says my mom.

Pam laughs a little.

"Uh oh," she says.

"What does that mean?" asks Dennis. "Too much partying?"

My parents are quiet.

"I suppose that depends on how you look at it," I say. Then I nod. "Yeah, probably too much partying."

Pam smiles. She looks warm and kind.

"What are you up to this summer?" she asks.

I open my mouth to say that I'm working at the park district. But I don't say that.

"I'm searching for someone," I say and then rip a piece off my biscuit and toss it in my mouth. I chew and then smile at her. "That's the interesting thing that I'm doing anyway. I'm also working my old summer job."

My mom furrows her brow. "Who are you searching for?" she asks.

"Adam Pazsitsky," I say.

"He's missing?" asks Dennis.

I nod. "Sort of. I saved his life about a week ago and now his mom says he's been missing since yesterday."

"You found him after he was hit by a car," says my dad. "You didn't save his life."

I shrug. There's silence at the table.

After dinner, I go out to the back porch to smoke. My parents are seeing me smoke for the first time this summer. They don't say anything about it but I can tell it upsets them. I try to do it out of sight.

Dennis opens the back door and steps outside. I can hear my parents talking to Pam as they clear plates and load the dishwasher. Dennis shuts the back door and sits down next to me on the porch stairs.

"How's it going?" he asks.

"Good," I say.

"When did you start smoking?"

"I guess I picked it up at school."

"Everything cool at school?"

I shrug.

"Pam's nice," I say.

"Yeah," he says.

"I feel like I can see your future together," I say.

Dennis gently scratches at something next to his eye.

"I hope I'm not that predictable," he says.

"You've got a good thing going."

He nods and I appreciate that he doesn't feel obligated to reciprocate the sentiment.

9.

The next day at work, I'm the one in a funk instead of John. I snap at him at the gardens while he stands next to the truck and smokes.

"You gonna stand there all day?" I ask.

"Jesus," says John, picking up his trowel. "What's your deal today?"

I look out the window as we drive back from the gardens. It's a grey day and there's a light drizzle, weak enough to continue working. John is listening to Radio Disney and smoking as he drives. I'm watching the mist of rain accumulate on the windshield only to be routinely sliced away by the wiper blade.

John turns down the radio.

"Hey, don't let me forget, I brought the tape for you."

"What tape?" I ask.

"The tape! Of me at the cemetery. Torturing Samuel with the other guys."

He says 'torturing' this time instead of 'goofing on.'

"Oh," I say. "Right."

By the time the workday ends, the clouds have cleared and the rain has stopped. The streets glisten in the sun.

I look down at the videotape in my hand as I walk home. The word 'Baseball' was written on the side sticker but has been scribbled over with black marker. I turn the tape over and over in my hands, wondering whether the contents of the tape will take me out of my foul mood or send me deeper into it.

Several blocks from home, I walk down the street that runs perpendicular to the Pazsitsky's block. I look over at their house and I notice that the branch is still at the curb and the front lawn still hasn't been mowed. I feel a pang of guilt even though I don't have anything to feel guilty about. I think about what I said at the dinner table the night before about searching for Adam. It was a stupid thing to have said but I feel an obligation to it now. I may not be saving the world like Dennis and Pam but I can at least try to help out someone like Adam.

Instead of going straight home, I walk down the block towards the Pazsitsky's. I cross the street and walk up their front steps. The screen door is caked in grey dirt but the front door behind it is open and I can hear the television playing. I look inside at the TV and can kind of make out one of those daytime self-help gurus. The rest of the house is unlit and I can only see the faint outline of furniture and, at the back of the house, windows through which the backyard can be seen. The backyard glows in contrast to the darkness inside the house.

I knock on the frame of the screen door.

"Hello?" I say.

After a moment, I hear the shuffle of footsteps on linoleum and the dark silhouette of Mrs. Pazsitsky moves against the background of the yard.

"Yes?" she asks as she stops the screen door. Maybe she can't see me well through the dirty screen.

"Hi. It's me again."

I can barely make out the details of her face behind the screen. There's that inscrutable face of hers resting on perpetually stooped shoulders. Her arm is in some type of sling.

"Yes?" she asks again.

I smile at her.

"They didn't take the branch," I say and motion with my thumb towards the curb.

She looks where I point.

"I guess not," she says.

Have you heard from Adam?" I ask. "Yesterday, you said you hadn't seen him in a while."

"No," she mumbles. "I haven't."

I want to ask whether she's reported his disappearance to the police but it doesn't seem like the right time.

"Okay," I say. "And how are you doing?"

"I'm fine," she says. I can't tell if she's intentionally being rude to me or if that's just her way.

"What happened to your arm?" I ask.

She looks down at it. "I strained a muscle trying to pull out that branch."

"Oh no,"

She opens her mouth to say something but hesitates. She looks behind me at the lawn.

"I was going to mow the lawn today. I feel so embarrassed by it but the doctor said I shouldn't move my arm. I tried mowing it with one arm—" She nods towards a corner of the lawn where there's a single zagging strip of mowed lawn. "It was too hard so I gave up."

"I'll mow the lawn," I say without hesitating.

"I wasn't trying to—"

"I don't mind," I say. "I do this type of thing all day. I'll finish in a flash."

I jog home from the Pazsitsky's. When I come in the back door, I see Dennis and Pam in the living room. Dennis is lying on the couch reading a book. Pam is sitting cross-legged on the large armchair reading what looks like a paper for school. They both look up at me when I come in the back door.

"Hey." Dennis puts down his book.

I walk into the living room.

"Hey," I say. I'm breathing heavy because of the jog home.

"What's up?" asks Dennis.

"Nothing," I say. "I'm going to mow the Pazsitsky's lawn."

Dennis gives me a curious look. "Why?"

"Because," I say. "Adam is gone and Mrs. Pazsitsky hurt her arm and can't do it herself."

Pam smiles. "That's nice," she says. "No word from Adam yet?"

"No." I almost tell her that I'm not sure whether I trust Mrs. Pazsitsky but I stop myself. That would sound ridiculous.

"What's that?" asks Dennis, looking at the tape in my hand.

"Oh," I say, holding it up. "A guy at work gave it to me."

"What is it?"

"It's a tape from his last job," I say. I laugh a little.

"What was his last job?" asks Pam.

"He was a gravedigger."

Dennis and Pam laugh.

"What's the tape of?" asks Dennis.

"It's..." I pause for a moment. "I don't know exactly. John said they used to harass this guy at work. He said it was hilarious. He recorded one of the pranks they played on him."

I waggle the tape in my hand. "That's what this is."

"Wow," says Dennis. Pam laughs again.

"Do you want to watch it?" I ask.

"Are you going to watch it now?" asks Dennis.

"No," I say. "But I will later."

Mrs. Pazsitsky leads me around back. The Pazsitsky's garage was probably white at one point but neglect has turned it the color of putty. As I pull up the garage door, we're hit with a sweet musty smell. We step inside.

"Adam's desk," mumbles Mrs. Pazsitsky, tapping an old desk pushed against the back of the garage. "He spent a lot of time out here."

There's a window above the desk that looks out into the leaves of an overgrown bush. The rest of the garage is antiquated in a way that I find pleasant. There's something about the smell of a garage that reminds me of my childhood.

"You don't have to do this," she says and I can tell she means it. It's almost as if she's asking me not to.

"I'm happy to."

I push the beat-up electric mower out to the front lawn. The lawnmower is old and low to the ground and one of the wheels is bent outward so the mower kind of wobbles.

I unwind the orange extension cord from around the handle of the mower and plug it into an old weatherproof outlet behind the front bushes. I pull back the mower handle and it starts up with a high-pitched buzz. This mower is far more quiet than the gas-powered mower we have at home.

After some trial and error, I discover the best way to cut the grass is with a rocking motion. Push the lawnmower about a foot forward and then pull backward. A wedge of grass is buzzed off with each back and forth lurch.

It's slow work and my arm muscles sting by the time I've finished the first two strips. I continue to work, strip by strip, hacking away at the lawn with the electric mower, flipping the extension cord out of my path with each turn completed.

I've never perspired much but it's a humid day and my shirt sticks to my sweat-covered back. Bugs float out of the grass like dandelion seeds. I slap at mosquitoes who take aim at my arms. I try to not regret volunteering. I consider returning home to get my parent's gas-powered lawnmower but the conditions of the task feel like a special challenge.

I rake the clippings into small piles then scoop the clippings into a refuse bag's drooping mouth. I feel a sense of accomplishment even though the lawn could look better. There are spots where I pushed the lawnmower too fast and left patches of tall grass.

I unplug the lawnmower and push it back up the driveway. I stand at the edge of the backyard and survey it. The grass back here is taller and thicker than the front lawn.

The sun is baking the top of my head. Cooking my brain, it feels like. I look at the house and wonder why Mrs. Pazsitsky hasn't come outside to offer me something to drink.

I step out of the sun into the shade of the garage. I walk to Adam's desk and drop into his chair. I take off my work gloves and rest them in my lap. I swivel around in the chair and look down the driveway towards the street, then swivel back around and look at the desk.

I open the bottom drawer. There's a wire-bound notebook with a yellow cover inside. I pick it up and flip through the pages. They're filled with a messy but legible cursive. This is a journal.

Without really thinking, I flip to the end of the journal and search for something about the night of the accident. I see the word 'quarry' and stop. I turn back a page and start reading.

I looked over at the clock. 10:45. A sad time. Not the saddest time though. Still early enough to do something. But what? Never anything to do but somehow everything to do. I put down my book. A bike ride. Why not? A nice nite.

I opened my door carefully, quietly. Looked across the hall at mom's door. There was light from the TV bouncing off the floor. Shifting around. I could hear the voices of characters talking behind the door. Good. A cover for sounds.

I walked to the first floor on the side of the stairs to keep them from creaking. Went around the edges of the kitchen so the floorboards wouldn't squeak. It worked again. Not a floorboard did creak. The back door was quiet as always. Only opened the door by about a foot. This is important otherwise the hinges will squeak.

Next was the screen door. The screen door is tricky. Almost unavoidably loud. The key is to open it very slowly. I spent maybe three minutes opening the door oh so slowly. I was patient. Finally got just enough room to slip through the door. With the screen door still open, I pulled the back door gently back into place. Then, just as slowly as I opened it, I slowly moved the screen door back into place. You have to be very patient with this part otherwise the hinges of the screen door will creak and that can be very loud.

The screen door did not make a noise until I let go of the latch. That made a click. Not too bad but I stopped and waited. Listened for mom moving above. Waited maybe two minutes but didn't hear anything from her.

I turned and went across the lawn to the garage. I have learned to step in a way that is quiet. I roll my feet. This way you are fast but quiet. I pretend I am floating and moving at a constant rate.

It was dark outside. Nice nitetime noises. Buzzing bugs. The moon broke through a cloud and the lawn got brighter. I looked up at Mom's window. Flickering blue light of the TV on the ceiling. That's all I could see from where I stood. TV on the ceiling.

Opened the garage door very slow, very quiet. Stepped inside. Shut my eyes, squeezed them shut. Kept them shut for like thirty seconds. Squeezing hard. When I opened them, voila! I could see in the dark. Roll-walked to my bike, picked it up, roll-walked it to the door. Walked the bike through the door. Did it carefully, made sure the pedals didn't catch on the door-frame.

I carried the bike down the driveway. Put it down on the street. Got on the bike and went for a ride. Warm night. Looked up at the sky. Some clouds in the sky but parts were clear. Can't see stars with the city so close. Light pollution. Just rode around. Nowhere in mind. Just moving to move. Looked at houses I passed, at people inside. Windows lit up like movie screens. Characters on a screen. Would like to listen in on them but just for a minute. Listen from a corner of the room. Leave after a minute. Forget it all happened tomorrow.

Rode to the quarry. Rode down the dark street that goes over it. I had an urge to see into it. Things like this can be sort of thrilling. I stopped and pulled my bike over the rail and into the tall weeds. Put the bike down and walked over to the fence. Climbed up to the top. Rust had eaten away at the barbed wire there. Was able to lean over the top of the fence, look down into the quarry. Down at the bottom was water. Far deep into it. Reflecting the moonlight.

Started thinking about how everything that had been in the quarry had been pulled out. The ground had been used to build things for us. To build sidewalks and streets and foundations. Just a big hole that some-

how became something that made our lives what they are. Remarkable and awful. Remembered hearing that a kid had thrown himself into the quarry. Imagined his fall to the bottom, the wind in his face, everything moving fast.

Stayed up on the top of that fence for maybe a minute but felt longer. Climbed down and took my bike out of the weeds. Started riding back down the street.

Heard a sound behind me. A car coming over the tracks. A big Cadillac rolled over the tracks. No headlights on. Something high school kids do. Drive down this road in the dark. I could hear loud music and people's voices and laughter from inside the car. Young voices. People maybe about my age. Maybe younger now.

The car was coming fast down the road. A cloud covered the moon and the road got darker.

My first thought: Get out of the road. Hop the rail into the weeds and wait for them to pass.

But I didn't. I stayed in the road.

Why? I felt anger. Immediate. At the car. At the people inside driving and laughing.

I decided that I would not be moved by them. I would continue as if they weren't there. I told myself: Make believe that they aren't there. Make believe that you are alone on this street.

I rode down the street, on my bike, with the big car barreling towards my back, but pretending that it wasn't.

I guess they didn't see me because they didn't stop. Maybe they were drunk. I was on the side of the street and maybe they didn't see me there. The road was very dark. I don't know why. I guess it was partially because they didn't have lights on. But I don't know why they didn't see me as they got closer. I guess they were talking to each other.

Their car moved up alongside me. I looked over at it. It was maybe an inch from my handlebar. I couldn't move any further from it without hitting the rail. I could feel the heat from the car. I could smell the oil from the engine. The passenger window moved up alongside me. It was open. I looked into it. There was a girl in there. My age. A little younger. She had brown hair and she was laughing at something that the driver had said.

I couldn't hear what he said but I could hear her laughter clear as a bell. The driver was another kid but I couldn't see his face from my angle. I could hear them perfectly but they couldn't hear me. Maybe because of the music.

The car hadn't touched me. It continued faster past me. I looked in the backseat as it passed. In the backseat were a number of people. Enough that they were sitting on one another's laps. Next to me was another girl. Chunkier, frizzy strawberry blonde hair. She was sitting on someone's lap and so she was higher in the seat. Her face was very high. Almost at the same level as me.

I looked over at her as she passed. She was laughing at something. Something that someone had said.

She turned and looked at me. Our eyes locked and there was a moment where I thought she didn't see me. But then she screamed. A loud blood-curdling scream. So loud that I instinctively pulled away from it. And as I did, my front tire hit the rail and my bike flipped forward and I could feel my stomach flip and my body flip.

I hear the the back door open. I fumble the journal back into the drawer and shut it. I jump up from the chair and walk out of the garage.

Mrs. Pazsitsky walks down the back steps, looking at me with that unreadable hardened expression. She's carrying a glass of water.

"Would you like some water?" she asks.

"Thanks," I say. I reach for the glass. My hand is shaking a little. We both notice.

I take a sip of the water. There's an odd taste to it, a faint flavor of dish soap maybe. The water looks foggy, maybe just air bubbles.

"I had to get out of the sun for a bit," I say.

She nods and watches me.

I raise my glass and gulp down the water. I'm wondering whether she can sense what I was doing in the garage. I feel the best thing for me to do is leave.

I finish the glass of water.

"It's getting really hot," I say. "Would you mind if I come back tomorrow?"

"You don't have to," she says.

10.

Lindsay and I meet at the gazebo next to the running path. The sun has almost set. There's a dark purple smudge along the horizon. We stretch under the lamplight next to the gazebo. Lindsay has an even brown tan that looks too good to be unintentional. She seems to sense that I am watching her as we stretch and she lunges deeper into her motions. It feels as though she's putting herself on display for me, though I don't want to assume that.

"Dennis is in town?" she asks, pushing against the lamppost, stretching her calf.

"Yeah," I say. I grab my ankle and pull backwards, stretching my thigh. I try not to look at Lindsay's butt as she stretches. She's wearing bright yellow running shorts which make her legs appear more brown.

"When did you become concerned about running alone at night?" I ask. "It never used to bother you."

"I don't know," she says, rocking into her calf stretch. "Did you know we were robbed?"

"No, you weren't," I say.

She laughs at my straightforward denial.

"Our garage was broken into," she says.

"That doesn't count."

We are quiet for a moment.

"Are you going to be able to seal our driveway this weekend?" she asks.

"Why?" I ask, frustration in my voice. "Does it need to get

done right away?"

"My dad wants it done this weekend. It's supposed to rain next week and he doesn't want to wait another week to finish it. If you're not going to do it then I'll get someone else to do it."

"I'll do it," I say. "I'll do it."

The path is dark where Lindsay and I run. There are lamp-posts but some are burnt out and they are spaced far enough from one another that we end up running through long stretches of darkness.

We both run as fast as we can. We don't talk. We listen to one another puffing out breaths and our feet scraping on the gravel.

We follow the path for several miles. It crosses over a street into the neighboring town. This is where we have turned around on past runs but my legs aren't tired. I feel as though I could run forever. I don't know where this energy has come from. Maybe I'm taking better care of myself now that I'm home for the summer. Maybe it's the frustration that I feel towards Lindsay.

"We should keep going," I say.

"You sure?" she asks.

"Yeah," I say.

We go another mile. Lindsay is not at her best today. I am setting the pace.

"Let's turn around at the factory," she says. There is an abandoned Ovaltine factory next to the path. It's a massive crumbling structure.

"I could go further," I say.

She pauses before responding.

"No," she says. "Let's turn around."

I feel great during the entire run back. When we near the gazebo, I ask her if she wants to do sprints.

"Fine," she says.

I point at a lamppost.

"From here to the next one," I say.

We ramp into a sprint as we pass the lamppost. Lindsay's footsteps drop off behind me. My stride feels wide and inexhaustible. I picture how I must look running and I'm impressed.

I reach the next lamppost and slow to a jog. I turn and watch Lindsay running towards me in the yellow lamp light. She looks weak, running the way an old woman would run.

After she passes the post, she bends over and puts her hands on her knees to catch her breath. I look at her running shorts and imagine pulling them off. I wonder whether she's tan underneath them. I jog towards Lindsay. As I reach her— my eyes still on her yellow shorts—her shoulders jerk and she vomits liquid into the grass.

"Whoa," I say, lurching backward. Lindsay wipes her mouth with her forearm.

"Sorry," she says.

11.

Dave sends John and me to the forest preserve that runs along the creek. There have been complaints about the amount of litter over there and we're supposed to clean it up.

"This is shit work," says John as we drive to the job. "Not our responsibility."

John's right. This job got dumped on us by the city because the higher paid maintenance guys didn't want to do it. As a type of rebellion against the job, John pulls the truck up over the curb and into the park. He drives across an empty baseball field and parks the truck as close to the woods as possible.

We put on work gloves and make our way through the forest with black garbage bags in hand. We pick up beer cans, spray paint canisters, fast food bags. We pass a burnt out camp fire with a broken fold-up lawn chair next to it. I pick up the lawn chair and force it into the bag.

I don't mind picking up this garbage. I try to imagine the people who used these things. I enjoy the work and, after a while, I can tell that John's enjoying himself too. He finds a waterlogged Playboy swollen to twice its thickness.

"Look at this!" John cries out and starts flipping through the pages, making loud grunts of appreciation. He makes the noises for my entertainment and I fake a chuckle.

I think about the forested area at the end of my block. Trees border each side of the running path. The foliage is thick enough that you can stand in there without being seen from the street or the path.

Growing up, our parents forbade us from going into the woods. For a while, there was a beat up beige couch in the woods that had been dragged in. Older kids would gather on it to smoke and drink.

Adam's older brother Mike was often down in the forest, hanging out on the couch. Mike was different from Adam. He had bright red hair and wore baggy shirts with the sleeves ripped off. There were bizarre stories about Mike. He thought it was funny to show people his asshole. He had bitten a teacher. I remember seeing him walk past our house once with a black eye that was starting to yellow around the edges. He seemed happy to have it. According to Dennis, Mike would often come to school drunk. He was eventually expelled and, shortly after that, he was gone. I imagine Mike's behavior stemmed from his dad. Mr. Pazsitsky was a truck driver who left one day for a job and never returned home.

Shortly before Mike dropped out, my neighborhood friends and I wanted to play hide and seek in the forest. We first wanted to check that no one was hanging out by the couch to bother us while we played. We walked to the edge of the woods and looked at the clearing where the couch was positioned.

"No one's there," someone said, but we all thought we heard muffled voices.

We stepped into the woods and rounded the couch slowly. A foot came into view. Then jeans, then a pale and pimply butt gyrating up and down. I saw a mane of red hair and the back of a black t-shirt. A thin arm with purple nail polish reached around and gripped the back of the shirt. We heard a loud moan which sent us running from the woods.

The next day, Mr. Donaldson and Mr. Langford went down to the park and pulled the couch out of the woods. I watched from my front yard as they dragged it up the Langford's drive-way. They broke the couch apart with a sledgehammer and left it at the curb for the garbagemen to carry away.

John and I come to the edge of the creek and stop. Both our bags are sagging with garbage. I look across the creek at a triangle of forested land; a hill surrounded on three sides by a tall fence, the highway, and the creek. It's a little urban island.

John sees me looking at it.

"I bet that's where people go to fuck," he says. "It's remote."

"Should we go over there?" I ask. There's no easy way to get to it. There are stones in the creek that we could hop across. That would be the easiest way.

"No," says John. "There's no garbage over there."

12

Mrs. Pazsitsky leads me around to the backyard again. She unlocks the garage with one hand and watches me as I roll out the lawnmower. I start to walk through the back yard, picking out sticks and rocks. She stands there and watches and then she walks up the back steps. She goes inside without saying anything to me.

I start up the mower and begin to push it through the grass. I notice Mrs. Pazsitsky through the window at the back of the house. She's sitting at the kitchen table and turning through the pages of a magazine. I expect she will eventually go away but she doesn't. She is still there after I've completed half the lawn, which takes almost an hour because of the thick grass and the poor condition of the mower.

I get the impression that I'm being watched and I decide to do a test. I stop the lawn mower and walk ahead of it towards a large stick that's in my path. In my periphery, I see Mrs. Pazsitsky's head raise up as I cross the lawn.

I bend down and pick up the stick and then toss it out of my path. I return to the mower and continue my work and her head moves back down to the magazine

I consider my options as I slowly push my way through the grass. The main reason that I came back today was to read more of Adam's journal. I could tell Mrs. Pazsitsky about the journal but she seems suspicious of me and that makes me suspicious of her. I would prefer to read the journal myself.

When I reach the back of the lawn, I notice a waist-high

strip of weeds and grass behind the garage and an idea comes to me which I act on without hesitation.

I stop the lawnmower and step into the weeds behind the garage. As soon as I'm out of Mrs. Pazsitsky's sightline, I run forward. I feel the sharp prick of thistle needles on my arms. A tree branch snags my shirt and I have to step backwards to get free from it.

I hurry through the weeds and turn down the other side of the garage. This side of the garage is laid with old paving stones. I run forward to the garbage cans and crouch down. I can smell something rotten inside the cans.

I look around the edge of the cans at the large window at the back of the house. Mrs. Pazsitsky is still behind the bay window. Her head is cocked forward. She is looking at the back of the lawn where I left the mower. I stay crouched behind the garbage cans and wait to see if she'll do anything.

She stands and walks away from the table. I am out of her sightline. I hurry into the open garage. I run to the desk and open the drawer with the journal in it. The drawer makes a squealing sound.

I hear the back door open. The journal is still there. I look at its yellow cover. I pull out the journal and slip into the back waist of my pants and then pull my shirt over it. I slowly close the desk drawer. It squeals again.

I walk with careful steps to the window on the side of the garage. I lean against the wall and look through the dirt-speckled window at the back door of the house. Mrs. Pazsitsky stands on the steps with her hand over her brow, shading her eyes so she can see to the back of the yard. It occurs to me that she could walk into the garage.

Mrs. Pazsitsky stands there for a moment and then walks down the back steps. As she steps towards the lawn, I take wide, quiet strides back towards the garbage cans. I turn the corner of the garage and run on the flat stones towards the back of it.

I turn the corner into the weedy strip behind the garage. I look towards the lawnmower and see Mrs. Pazsitsky's shadow growing larger on the grass as she gets closer. I reach down and grope for something in the weeds. My hands land on a large rock. I wrap my fingers around it. It's heavy and cool in my hand. I see a fallen tree branch and pick that up with my other hand.

I hear Mrs. Pazsitsky's footsteps stop as she reaches the back of the garage. I stand erect. I hold up the branch and the rock.

"Look at these," I say, maybe a little too loudly.

Mrs. Pazsitsky looks at me. The sunlight is hitting her from the side and I can't see her eyes in the shadow of her brow. She is quiet for a moment.

"Wouldn't want to run over these with the mower," I say into the silence, chuckling.

"You don't have to do back here," she says.

"I don't mind," I say, dropping my arms to my waist.

"It's very weedy," she says.

I take several steps forward and glance at the mower.

"The mower does seem a little stressed. Let me go to the hardware store to get a new blade for it."

"No," she says. "It won't last much longer."

"Alright," I say.

Mrs. Pazsitsky turns and walks back towards the house. I drop the rock and branch into the grass.

I feel the journal pressed against my back as I walk home. I wonder whether it's noticeable and keep trying to glimpse my reflection in the windows of passed houses but I can't get a good view. As I walk, I feel the journal kind of working its way up my waistline but I don't stop and readjust out of concern that someone might see me.

When I get home, I find Dennis and Pam on the back porch sitting in plastic deck chairs. They look at me as I come up the back walk. I feel the bottom of the notebook riding up my belt line. It's tipping away from my back.

"Hey," says Dennis.

"Hey," I say and force a smile.

"We were just talking about you," he says. "We're bored. Could we watch that tape?"

"Which tape?" I ask.

"Of your co-worker," says Dennis.

"The gravedigger," adds Pam. She smiles at me.

I had forgotten about the tape.

"Sure," I say, eager to be away from their eyes. "Let me grab it."

I'm trying to sound normal but I can't tell if it's working. I wonder if Dennis and Pam are watching me as I mount the back steps. I catch my reflection in the glass of the porch door and notice a bump at the back of my shirt where the fabric has tented around the journal. The bump isn't glaring but it would be noticeable if someone's eyes happened to fall on it.

In my bedroom, I pull the journal out from the back of my pants and toss it on the bed. My sweat has turned the cardboard backing a dark brown. My hands are trembling. I shake them in the air. I walk back and forth next to my bed and blow out a breath.

I snatch up the the journal from my bed and look at the cover. I pick up the edge of the notebook with my thumb and flip through the pages. The cursive handwriting blurs past my eyes. I open my dresser drawer, pull out John's tape, and put the journal in the drawer. I shut the drawer and go back downstairs.

13

"I don't know what this will be like," I say as I push the tape into the VCR. "It could be fun or it could be disturbing."

"Or both," says Dennis.

"We hope," says Pam.

I hit play and then sit on the couch beside Dennis and Pam. There's a brief flicker of a baseball game and there's a crackling sound and the baseball field is rolled over by a bouncing image of someone walking with the camera pointed at the grass. The tape stabilizes and the soft sound of the feet moving through grass mixes with the sound of wind hitting the camera mic.

The camera swings upward and a clumsy auto-focus reveals a man in his early fifties standing in front of a rundown utility garage. Trees surround the garage. Behind the trees is a large field of grass and then further back are gravestones. The man stands in front of an open garage door.

The quality of the tape is terrible. The sky in the background is blown out and the shadows are more brown than black.

The man stands next to a dirt-covered mini-excavator. I assume this is Samuel. He has the air of a quiet man. He's older than I expected, more normal and dimensional. The man who John described was a cartoon; this man is not. He wears a trucker's hat tipped back on his head. He wears large bifocals, his eyes are small and cautious behind the glasses. He has a potbelly.

The person holding the camera stops and trains the camera on Samuel. They are maybe fifteen feet from one another. Samuel looks off in the distance, away from the camera, though his eyes keep sneaking sidelong glances at it. Behind the camera, and loud on the audio track, comes the sound of chuckling. It sounds like John's laugh but it's not the laughter I'm accustomed to hearing from him. It's more sinister and vicious.

The camera stays on Samuel for a while. I keep waiting for something to happen but it doesn't. The camera just stays on him.

I glance over at Dennis and Pam sitting next to me. Pam is cuddled under Dennis's arm. She's smiling but also gripping Dennis's arm the way one might at a horror film. Dennis appears calm and attentive.

I look back at the screen.

Samuel says something but he's too far away to be heard. His voice is just a thin murmur. Then loud laughter from John behind the camera. "Say that again!" John calls out to Samuel. His voice is so loud that it distorts.

Samuel doesn't repeat himself. He just shakes his head 'no.'

There is a sudden spasm of laughter from John as a man in a grey shirt darts out of the garage behind Samuel. The laughter is so loud that I start. The man lunges at Samuel's jeans. At first I think the man will tackle Samuel. Instead, he tries to pulls down Samuel's pants. Samuel leaps away and grabs his waistband, a move executed so quickly and instinctively that a history of past attempts can be sensed.

The man who ran out of the garage has a big, goofy grin. He stumbles a little as he passes Samuel and almost falls down. He plays up this stumble for the camera. He veers close to the camera and, as he passes it, we get a glimpse of him. He has shaggy black hair and one of his front teeth is crooked. He seems both embarrassed and energized by the camera.

The camera turns back to Samuel who still stands in front of the garage but now further away from the open door. Samuel appears calm despite the attempted de-pantsing. He has his hands in his pockets now.

Samuel is not the simpering idiot who John has described. If anything, Samuel seems composed and patient. He's certainly more likable than John or the guy with the crooked tooth.

John takes several steps forward and starts calling out questions to Samuel. Odd questions designed to provoke a reaction.

"What's your name?" John asks.

Samuel's lips move with a response that the camera doesn't pick up.

"Now that's not your real name. What's your real name?"

Samuel ignores the question.

"Who do you live with?" asks John.

Samuel continues to look off in the distance. For some reason, I assume Samuel must still live with his mother.

John keeps repeating these questions, waiting for a reaction, but he doesn't get one. The bouncing camera is unsettling and I start to feel queasy.

There's a thumping noise as John fumbles with something on the camera. A sharp zoom and suddenly we're much closer to Samuel. John quietly tapes Samuel in medium close-up for several minutes. We all study the details of Samuel's face and dress as he stares off silently into the distance.

"This is kind of boring," I say. Dennis and Pam laugh.

I raise the remote and press fast forward. We zip through much of the same. Several minutes of John's life spent bothering another person, now at four times the speed.

Then there is a flurry of movement. The man in the grey shirt comes running after Samuel again. The camera bounces around and the image becomes unreadable.

"Looks like something is happening," says Dennis.

I hit play. John's laughter and the sound of rustling fabric bursts out of the speakers. The camera swings towards the opening of the garage and then bounces around as John runs forward. The man in the grey shirt chases Samuel into the darkness. John follows in. "Get him," he yells.

The camera can't pick up anything in the garage except vague dark movements. Over the obscure image is John's grating and ecstatic laughter. John keeps yelling 'Get him.'

After a while, John stops calling out and the only sound is feet shuffling on cement and the only thing visible are dark blurs of movement.

"This is kind of disturbing," says Pam and all three of us laugh.

After several minutes of shuffling sounds, John starts to laugh again. He and his camera walk out into the light of the day. The lens flares at the brightness then the exposure auto-adjusts.

John puts the camera down on the mini-excavator and the camera racks focus to the yellow paint on the side of it. The detail of the yellow paint seems sharp and bright after the darkness of the garage. John keeps laughing. He sounds so pleased. This must be the greatest day of his life.

There's a crackling sound and a flicker of blue and then the baseball game begins again. It's a day game. We see the baseball field and then cut to a baseball player standing outside the batter's box. The announcer flatly relays statistics as the batter tugs on his gloves and readjusts his helmet before stepping up to the plate.

"I guess that was it," I say as I stand and hit eject on the remote.

"Huh," says Dennis.

"Yeah," I say. "A little bit of a bust. John said that would be the best thing I've ever seen."

"I don't know about that," says Dennis. "It was interesting though."

"Kind of," I say.

14.

I finish reading Adam's journal and close it. I look out the window at the trees and the streetlights. A thought starts working around my brain. Adam seemed depressed about his life. His journal made numerous mentions of feeling watched and wanting to escape. When Adam was looking down into the quarry, he imagined being the kid who had jumped into it. There isn't anything explicit in the journal. He never directly mentions suicide but I have a hard time escaping the possibility of it.

I decide to go for a walk. Downstairs, I find Dennis in the kitchen cutting up an apple. I hear the shower running in the bathroom.

"What are you up to?" he asks.

"Just going for a walk. Wanna come?" I ask.

"Sure," he says.

As we walk around the block, Dennis talks about Lindsay; he talks about the fellowship that she's applied for and how she's nervous about whether she'll get it. I only partially listen to him. I'm nagged by the idea of Adam's journal and the idea of him killing himself. I can't tell whether I'm being irrational and I want to get Dennis's opinion but I don't know how to bring it up without it seeming like I don't care about what he's talking about.

"Everything alright?" Dennis asks, sensing my distraction.

I hesitate for a moment.

"Actually," I say. "No."

I tell him about stealing the journal from the Pazsitsky's garage. I realize the childishness of these actions as I say them but I justify my actions by explaining that Mrs. Pazsitsky seemed calm and unaffected by Adam's disappearance. I tell him what Adam says about his mom in the journal.

"He says she sleepwalks through her days, barely speaks. She just watches whatever's on TV. No friends, just her cashier job."

I tell about Adam's refrains to escape, to be away from other people.

"He says he wants to get away?" asks Dennis.

"Yeah," I say. "But he doesn't say where. I don't know how he'd escape. He couldn't get a job; he was too awkward and introverted. He didn't want to go to college even though he was probably smart enough for it. He doesn't strike me as someone who could travel. When someone wants to escape but can't manage the outside world, where do they go?"

Dennis shrugs. "Deeper inside?"

"I feel somehow responsible for him," I say.

"What are you going to do with the journal?" he asks. I can tell Dennis wants me to return the journal and tell Mrs. Pazsitsky about it but he doesn't want to suggest it outright. Instead, he will try to lead me to that conclusion myself. I don't want to give him the satisfaction of that.

"I don't know," I say. "Maybe I'll just sneak it back into place."

15

Later that night, as I lie in bed, my mind turns to Adam. For whatever reason, I recall this memory that I have of him. Nothing important, I don't think, but it stuck with me. The time I'm thinking of was early on in the seventh grade.

It wasn't basketball season yet so I didn't have to stay after school for practice. I had walked home through the chill of early fall. Normally someone was home at our house, either my brother or one of my parents, but the house was empty that day. The silence inside the house and the overcast weather made the house feel especially lonely and I decided to go for a walk to get away from it.

I walked down the block towards the park. I walked slowly and took in the scenery along the way; I looked at the wet bark of the trees and the grey sky which seemed just a few shades lighter than the sidewalk. I observed my breath fogging before me. The fall weather had sent me into a funk, as it often does, but the walk seemed to help.

At the end of the end of the block, I walked up the narrow incline to the wooded area that runs the length of the park. I walked alongside the woods with my hands in the pockets of my hoodie. Squirrels darted away as they heard me shuffling through the damp leaves.

I came to the gravel path that curves around the woods and up over the railroad tracks to the other side of the park. As I approached the path, I heard the popping dribble of a basketball and the metallic clang of a ball bricking on the rim.

I walked up over the tracks and looked down at the basketball court and saw Adam Pazsitsky down there practicing by himself. He was wearing a dirty white tee shirt that was much too big for him. I walked along the path and watched Adam as he practiced. Adam's back was towards me and he didn't notice me watching him.

Adam stopped at the free throw line and took a jump shot. His form was a little off. He threw the ball straight from his chest which killed the arc of the shot. The ball bricked hard. He rebounded it and took another shot a few feet from the hoop which also bricked and sailed far from the hoop.

"Jesus," I whispered and chuckled at Adam's missed shots.

Adam retrieved the ball and jogged back to the court and then dribbled to the top of the key. Adam had a funny crouched way of dribbling, hovering over the ball like it was an animal about to escape. He stopped behind the three-point line and leaned forward, readying himself for something.

Adam waited a moment, focusing himself, and then charged forward, dribbling just inside the three point line. He then hooked a shot over his head. The shot was flat and ugly but it went in.

I stayed and watched Adam for a few minutes. He lined up again at the free throw line. Once again, Adam charged along the far side of the court and hooked the shot over his head. Once again, it flew in almost a straight line towards the basket and dropped through the hoop. I stood there and watched Adam do this shot four times and, amazingly, the shot went in each time. I had thought Adam making the shot had simply been a fluke but I could see that it was actually some special shot that he had mastered.

I was surprised by Adam's shot but it somehow made sense. Adam could pull off the ugly shot which you never thought would sink but a conventional jump shot was something he just couldn't figure out.

16.

I put on old running shoes and a pair of shorts that I don't mind getting dirty. I leave the house and start towards the Cookes. It's a beautiful day and I'm a little resentful that I have to spend it sealing a driveway. I remind myself to keep a good attitude. I ask myself what else I would be doing if not this. This justification doesn't quite work. I'm sure I would find something to do.

When I get to the Cookes, I walk up the long driveway and ring the front doorbell. I look around as I wait. The front porch is really something to behold. There's perfectly-laid flagstones and a birdbath that's bubbling up water. Around the edges of the porch is an elaborate and lush array of flowers.

Mr. Cooke answers the door. His white hair seems to be gleaming today. He's wearing a periwinkle polo tucked into khaki shorts. His sculpted legs are tan and almost hairless. I'm reminded how short he is; a thought which he seems to read on my face.

"Hi," I say.

"Hi," he says. He doesn't smile.

"Just a moment." He shuts the door and leaves me on the porch. After waiting several minutes, I sit down on the wrought iron bench and watch birds flit to and from the birdbath. Mr. Cooke returns a few minutes later.

"Okay," he says, shutting the door behind him.

He walks past me and expects that I'll follow, like an obedient dog or something. I stand up and follow him, though the idea of walking away or staying where I am crosses my mind and gives me a sort of pleasure.

I follow him back to the side door of the garage. He pulls out a pair of keys and unlocks several locks.

"High security," I say.

"Someone was stealing food from the fridge," he mutters.

"You have a refrigerator in your garage?"

"Yes," he says as he opens the door.

He grabs some necessary tools. A push broom, a driveway squeegee, a screwdriver. He hands these tools to me.

"Here," he says and looks me in the eyes. "Take these."

He lifts a bucket of sealant by the handle and starts towards the garage door. He stops and looks down at my legs.

"You're wearing shorts," he says.

"Right," I say. I almost explain that I don't have any pants that I'd be willing to ruin but I use a minimal amount of explanation because that's what he seems to be doing to me.

"You'll want to wear pants," he says and looks towards the house. "I could get you a pair of mine."

"It's okay," I say. "I'll be fine."

He looks at my legs, considering.

"Your pants would be too small for me," I add. "Unless you have sweatpants."

"Alright," he says and picks up the can of sealant. I smile, glad that I was able to get in a dig at his size.

At the front of the driveway, he puts the bucket of sealant on the grass and takes the broom from me.

"This is how you'll want to do it," he says.

He moves with brisk assuredness, sweeping off the first few feet of the drive with sharp, fast pushes. I am impressed. For someone who I associate with privilege, Mr. Cooke seems comfortable with physical labor. He moves with a speed and determination that seems almost savage. As he kneels down and uses the screwdriver to pry the lid off the can of sealant, I'm reminded of the stories that circulate about him. His forceful movements and minimal words make me think the stories must be true.

"You'll just want to put a little down," he says as he steps back and pours the black liquid onto the driveway. He keeps the bucket far from him as he pours. The dark soup splatters as it hits the driveway and a few speckles of sealant get onto his shoes. He notices the speckles but keeps moving.

He picks up the driveway squeegee and pushes the thick liquid around, careful at the edges of the drive so that it doesn't bleed over onto the sidewalk.

He stops demonstrating and hands me the driveway squeegee.

"You won't finish the whole driveway today. Try to get half done. You can do the second half tomorrow."

"Okay," I say.

He looks down at my legs. I see amusement dance in his eyes.

"Are you sure you don't want a pair of pants?"

"No thanks," I say. "I'll be fine."

I sweep off half the driveway then start pouring sealant. On the first pour, the sealant splashes onto my shoes.

"Shit," I mutter.

I slowly work my way up the drive. With each pour, more and more of the sealant splashes onto me. It covers my shoes and socks. It gets up onto my legs, coating my skin in erratic splashes of black. It doesn't matter how far I hold the bucket from me. I start to wonder if maybe my effort to keep the sealant off my legs is somehow making me more susceptible to it.

I try to match the efficiency of Mr. Cooke but I can't. There are too many considerations to juggle and I don't want to make a mistake. I'm trying to spread the sealant evenly but I don't know how much is the right amount. I don't want to get the sealant on the grass but I move too slow when I'm careful. I try not to step on the spread sealant but I repeatedly do as I try to move quick.

Thankfully, I don't see Lindsay while I'm working. If she came outside and saw me with my legs covered in sealant then I would have to mask my embarrassment by playing it for laughs. She would laugh and I'm sure she wouldn't care but this underlying knowledge would be there: I don't know what I'm doing.

Around one, I get to the halfway point and decide to stop. I put the lid on the bucket of sealant and I walk the tools up the driveway. I'm debating whether I should walk up the steps of the back porch to knock and let Mr. Cooke know that I'm done for the day when the back door opens.

"All done?"

"Well, half of it," I say.

He looks down at my legs.

"What are you going to do about that?" he asks.

I look down. The sealant has dried. My shins and feet are caked in a dull black shell that is somehow both hard and flexible.

"You don't think soap and water will take it off?" I ask.

Mr. Cooke looks at me flatly.

"No," he said. "I'm not sure what will. Gasoline might."

"I'll try that when I get home," I say.

"Wait," he says and walks past me down the steps and into the garage. He pulls out a red tin of gasoline and a rag. He pours gasoline on the rag and hands it to me. I've always liked the smell of gasoline but it's too much when it's this close. It makes my eyes water and my stomach turn.

"Try that," he says.

I rub the gasoline on my legs. The black coating smears and bleeds into the rag. It clears a spot in the sealant and my skin becomes visible.

"Looks like it's working," I say.

Mr. Cooke looks at my legs and nods. He seems to be doing some sort of mental calculation that I can't figure out.

"You can use that to clean it off," he says. "Just leave the gas can by the tools when you're done. I'll put them away."

He walks back into the house. I spend the next fifteen minutes rubbing gasoline on my body. After clearing off the sealant, I inspect my shins. I notice tiny black specks in the pores. I try to clear out the specks by pinching and scraping at them but they don't move. It's like the sealant has burrowed into my skin.

17.

I wake up before my alarm clock. My eyes are sore for some reason. When I get out of bed, I notice Adam's yellow journal on my dresser. I still haven't returned it. I tell myself that I will do it tomorrow. I walk down to the first floor and out to the back yard. I pick up the sealant encrusted shorts and shoes that I let dry in the grass overnight.

When I get to the Cookes, I find the tools set out for me in front of the garage. I look at the house but don't see any lights on inside. I bring the equipment down to where I stopped yesterday. The sun starts to rise above the trees surrounding the property. It's going to be a hot day. Of course, I didn't bring any sunblock with me.

I sweat a little as I sweep off the driveway. I notice my legs tingling.

I put on my gloves and pry open the can of sealant. I look down at the thick black liquid in the bucket. It seems pure and condensed. I wonder if it tastes how it smells. Some part of my brain wants to drink it. I stand and pour the sealant onto the driveway. It splashes onto my shoes. I don't care. They're already ruined.

I start to push the sealant across the driveway with the squeegee. I enjoy the way the light bounces off it; shiny, like the skin of the seal printed on the side of the bucket.

The sun is over the tops of the trees now. My shadow is sharp on the ground. I'm sweating more. The tingling in my legs is more intense. It's turned into a hot itch. It originates deep under the skin. I tell myself it's just a minor reaction to the sealant or maybe the gasoline, but the irritation cannot be ignored. It's sharp and it burns. It feels like sweat is trapped under my pores, boiling in my skin. I have to fight an instinctive urge to drop the squeegee handle and furiously scratch my legs. I sense that once I start itching, I won't stop.

After several minutes of ignoring the pain, I rest the squeegee on the grass. With forced calmness, I take off my work gloves. Instead of scratching, I rub my palms over the areas that itch. This temporarily relieves the itch but the itch is replaced with a burning sensation.

I walk across the lawn into the shade of an evergreen. I want to run but I force myself to walk. Under the shade of the evergreen, I scratch at the skin on my legs. For a moment, the itch is gone, but it returns. I scratch again, so hard that skin bunches up under my fingernails. There are red streaks on my legs. The burning seems to subside after several minutes in the shade. I walk back towards the driveway. The itch returns.

"Fuck," I hiss.

I try to ignore the irritation. I put on my gloves and set back to work. There are moments where my mind seems to have filtered it out but then a stab of burning pain returns, so sharp that I grunt. I have to scratch.

I consider my options. I could tell Mr. Cooke that I can't seal his driveway because I didn't accept his offer for pants yesterday. Or I could push my way through the agonizing irritation, stopping every thirty seconds to grit my teeth and scratch at my legs. I choose the latter and continue to work, muttering curses under my breath.

A thought occurs to me. This is karmic payback for stealing Adam's journal. I shouldn't have stolen it. I should have returned it to Mrs. Pazsitsky several days ago. This is my punishment. I need to return the journal as soon as possible. My legs will burn like this until I return it to Mrs. Paszitsky and tell her what I have read.

After thirty minutes, my legs are bright pink and I've made scant progress. I stop and look up the driveway at all the ground that I need to cover today. It seems unlikely I will finish. I turn back to my work and I see Lindsay walking towards me from the sidewalk. She's wearing her workout clothes, those yellow shorts and a race tee shirt.

Lindsay smiles as she approaches but she doesn't look pleased to see me. The last time I saw her was when we went for a run and I outran her. A brief feeling of pride comes over me.

"Hey," she says.

"Hey." I ignore the painful needles in my legs.

"How's it coming?" she asks.

"It's alright," I say.

"My legs really itch right now," I say, gritting my teeth.

"What from?" she asks.

"I don't know," I say. I reach down and scratch at my legs with the gloves. "Either the sealant or the gasoline that I used to remove it from my legs. I think maybe the sealant plugged up my pores. The pain only started when I got in the sun."

"It hurts?" she asks.

"It kills."

"Come inside. I'll get you something for it."

She steps towards the house. I look at her, considering whether I should follow.

"My shoes," I say.

"Just take them off."

I stay where I am.

"It's fine," she says. "Come on."

"Is your dad home?" I ask.

She looks at the house. "I don't know," she says. "I don't think so. I don't think anyone is home."

I feel a sharp needle of pain.

"Alright," I say and I walk towards the back of the house with her.

I take off my shoes and socks and leave them on the driveway next to the back door. We go inside. The house is refreshing. Ceiling fans circulate cool air around the rooms.

My mind momentarily goes back to Adam and I let out a sigh. Lindsay looks back at me as we walk through the house. She smiles.

"You okay?"

"I'm alright," I say. I'm silent as I think. I consider whether I want to tell Lindsay about the situation with Adam. For some reason, part of me wants to tell her. If I do then whatever leverage I might have over her from the run will be nullified.

"Did I tell you about Adam?"

"Who?

"Pazsitsky. I didn't then."

"No."

I take a deep breath and start to tell her the story from the beginning. I leave out the part about wanting to one-up Dennis and Pam at the dinner table. I turn the story so that it makes me sound a little more reasonable. Lindsay seems to sense my manipulation of events. She can tell that I've done something foolish which doesn't seem to surprise her.

We get to the upstairs bathroom before I finish the story. Lindsay has me sit on the edge of the tub and hands me a bottle of aloe vera.

"Put that on," she says.

"Alright," I say. I flick the top of the bottle against my palm so all of the green goop slops towards the nozzle. I uncap the bottle and start to apply the aloe to my legs and, as I do, I tell Lindsay the rest of the story. I tell her about Adam's numerous journal entries about wanting to escape. I see a look of genuine concern on her face.

"Do you think he killed himself?" she asks.

"I don't know," I say. "He never says it explicitly."

She shakes her head.

"Why aren't you laughing at this story?" I ask. "You look so serious."

"It's a sad story."

"It's the type of story that would have made you laugh when we were together."

"It's not funny."

She leans against the sink and watches me as I rub the gel on my legs.

"Why did you take the journal?" she asks.

"I don't know," I say. "I was curious."

She looks at me in a way that reminds me of her dad.

"You can't do dumb things like that forever," she says.

Sitting on the tub in the bathroom and rubbing the gel on my legs makes me feel like a child. I almost tell her that I was trying to help him but that's not exactly true so I stop myself. I continue to rub the stuff on my legs.

"I know," I say. "I know."

18.

A downpour starts that night. The rain bullets the the side of our house and rolls down windows in thick sheets that look like syrup. The shallow end of our block pools with water. I sit in the living room and watch the storm. I see Mr. Flaherty walk down the block in waders and a yellow slicker. He brings a metal rake with him. The Flaherty's basement filled with rain water during the big flood. Now he stands sentry at the shallow end of the block whenever there's a storm and pushes debris away from the sewer grates.

It's still raining the next day. I've never seen it rain so hard for so long.

At breakfast, my mom stares out the window with a look of disgust on her face.

"Look at this," she mutters, referring to the rain.

"Quarry's almost full," says my dad. He turns a page of the newspaper.

"Really?" I ask.

The rain finally starts to let up late in the afternoon and I call Lindsay.

"This is a bad idea," she says.

"His body would be floating at the top of it. No one else is going to check."

"Did you return the journal?" she asks.

"I will," I say.

She's quiet. Like me, I imagine she's eager to be out of the house.

"Let's say his body is there, what will you do?" she asks.

"I doubt it's there. If it's there then I'll go to the police."

"And if it's not?"

"Then we get to see the inside of the quarry at night."

To my amazement, she agrees.

I park in the Cooke's driveway and look at the blacktop. It looks nice and smooth. This satisfies me. I walk to the front door and find it partially open. I push it open the rest of the way and step into the dark foyer. I think of Adam when he walked into that stranger's house.

I see the flickering light of a TV at the back of the house. I walk towards it. I find Mr. Cooke in the living room. He's sitting on the couch, watching a news program. I watch him from behind. He seems to sense my presence and looks over his shoulder. He starts when he sees me.

"Jesus," he gasps.

"Sorry," I say. "The front door was open. I'm just picking up Lindsay."

He sighs and looks back at the TV. I look at what he's watching.

"Driveway looks good," I say.

"I hear you had some trouble with your legs."

I'm quiet. Of course he had to bring this up. I want to challenge him on this, maybe somehow bring up his shady past. Instead, I go into the dark front room, sit on the couch, and wait for Lindsay to come downstairs.

19.

We park on a quiet street next to the train tracks. It has stopped raining but everything in the world is still wet and dripping. I grab the flashlight and shut the car door. We walk across the tracks towards the quarry. We don't see any cars or people. Maybe they're waiting for the rain to pick up again.

"Thanks for doing this," I say.

Lindsay nods.

I think about what Mr. Cooke said to me back at her house.

"Did you tell your dad about what happened with my legs?" I ask.

She's quiet.

"I mentioned it to him. Why?"

I sigh.

"I wish you hadn't."

"Why? He doesn't care."

We come down the other side of the tracks and walk towards the chainlink gates. The gate is padlocked. Behind the fence are the old offices and the abandoned processing plant.

"I don't think we'll be able to get in this way," says Lindsay.

We walk past the entrance along the street where I found Adam. There are no lights here. I recall Adam writing that a portion of the barbed wire had rusted away. I see where he's referring to.

"There," I say, pointing.

Lindsay squints her eyes.

"It's rusty," she says.

I ignore her comment and step over the guardrail into the weeds. I push my way towards the fence. The weeds are wet and I feel the water soaking through my jeans. I look back at Lindsay. She sighs and steps over the guardrail. I pull myself up the fence and look over at the other side. I'm about to flip my leg over the top of the fence when I see headlights approaching from beyond the tracks. I hurry back down.

"Someone's coming." We both crouch down into the weeds. A tall weed flicks me in the face and water sprays into my eyes. I wipe my face across my shoulder. I hear Lindsay mutter something under her breath.

The car comes over the tracks. It's a large SUV and its bright lights illuminate everything around us for a moment. The shadows cast from the weeds rotate past us as the car continues down the road. We stand up once we see red taillights receding. I look through the fence at the other side.

"It looks clear over there," I say. "You go first."

I expect Lindsay will protest but she doesn't. She sighs and pulls herself up the fence. I keep waiting for her to back out of this. I can tell that she doesn't really want to be here, that she thinks this is a ridiculous idea, but she doesn't say no and I like her for that.

Lindsay climbs up the fence, flips over the top, and climbs down the other side. She does this with fluid dexterity and I'm reminded that she's in excellent condition. She's not embarrassed or self-conscious as she moves. She's focused on the task and she's comfortable enough with me that she doesn't even seem to consider it. She wipes her hands on her shorts as she walks away from the fence, looking around at the front drive and the processing plant. I swing over the top of the fence and let myself down the other side.

Lindsay has walked into the center of the large drive that leads into the quarry.

"Your family built this," I say.

"Yeah," she says.

"Have you been here before?" I ask.

"I came a few times when I was a kid."

We walk past the processing plant towards the quarry. The moon is out but it's blocked by lingering storm clouds. We stop at the edge and look down. It's a sheer drop of about twenty feet to the water. Lindsay looks at me.

"Are you going to use the flashlight?" she asks.

I glance behind me.

"Aren't you afraid that someone will see it?" I ask.

"What did you come here for if we aren't going to look?"

I turn back to the water and pull out the flashlight. I click it on and point it down at the water. I don't know what to expect in there, floating debris or something, but there's nothing, just the dark water. I move the beam along the edge. I point the flashlight towards the center of the water but the light weakens at this distance and the water looks like dark nothingness.

"I don't know what it would look like if his body were floating," I say.

I look at Lindsay and she shrugs.

"Let's walk along the edge," she says.

This surprises me. I was expecting we would just stand at the edge of the quarry and run the flashlight across the surface of it. Lindsay wants to go further into this than I do. I wonder if she's testing me. Maybe this is a game of chicken. Maybe she wants to see who will relent first and show fear. The way running with one another was a type of game.

Lindsay walks over to where the fence runs along the edge of the quarry. I follow behind her. There's about a foot of space between the fence and the drop into the quarry. Lindsay grabs onto the chainlink and starts stepping her way through the weeds.

I tuck the flashlight into my back pocket and follow her. The weeds come up to my hips and I can't see my feet. Each step feels like a gamble that we'll step on a living creature or the ground will crumble beneath us. A car passes behind the fence but we don't stop moving. I look around the edge of the quarry. It's a long wrap around and I wonder if we're going to go the entire way.

"Hang on a sec," I say.

Lindsay stops. I click on the flashlight and point it down at the water. I move the beam slowly across the surface. Part of me expects to see a body and part of me knows it won't be there.

"What are you going to do if we find him?" asks Lindsay.

"Tell the police."

I stop my light on something. I stare down at it. It's a bump on the surface of the water. Difficult to make out.

"Oh Jesus," I say.

Lindsay looks down at the water.

I keep the flashlight on it for a moment. It's hard to decipher. It looks like a piece of clothing with air trapped underneath it.

"What is it?" asks Lindsay.

"I'm not sure," I say.

"Is that him?" she asks. I hear panic in her voice. Something zaps between us. A shared shame over our callousness. A realization that we're totally unequipped to handle what we're searching for. We will have to deal with the death of someone; we will be close to it. Our actions will ripple in people's lives.

"I don't know," I say.

I keep the light on it and we both silently inspect the shape, trying to decipher what we're looking at. It's difficult to tell. I try to think of things it could be; I wait for it's nature to suddenly become apparent but the object can't solidify in mind.

"We should try poking it or something," I say. "Try to turn it over"

"It's too far away."

She's right. It's a far reach from where we're at. I couldn't even come close to it with a branch.

"Fuck," I whisper.

I look over at Lindsay. I watch her squinting down at it.

"It's a plastic bag," she says.

"Are you sure?" I ask.

She nods.

"Yeah."

20.

I walk down the sidewalk. The world looks excellent today. The sun has burnt off all the rainwater. The grass is tall and verdant. The flower petals are saturated with color. I'm not appreciating it, though. I look down at Adam's journal in my hands as I walk to the Pazsitsky's.

I walk up their front steps. I hear the television inside. I knock on the screen door. There's a squeak of couch cushions as someone rises to answer the door. Mrs. Pazsitsky shuffles towards me. Her face and glasses barely register behind the dirty screen.

"Hi," I say. "How's your arm?"

"Okay," she says.

I try to see her face as something more than just an unresponsive sad sack of skin. I'm sure she has complex emotions but I can't picture what they'd look like on her face.

"Well," I say, clearing my throat and looking down at the journal in my hand. "I came over because I wanted to tell you about something."

I breathe in and start my explanation. I tell her about taking the journal from the garage and reading it. I offer justifications; I try to paint myself as sincere and concerned but it doesn't ring true. I tell her about reading the journal, that some of the entries worried me. I don't tell her about the quarry or the object floating in the water. Why bother? It almost certainly was a plastic bag.

She stares at me during the whole explanation. She doesn't

move her head. Her eyes are like small raisins behind her glasses. When I finish, I hold out the journal in front of me. She's quiet for a moment. She pushes open the screen door and takes the journal. She looks down at it and then back at me.

"Adam's fine," she says.

"Oh," I say, uncertain how to respond. "That's good."

"I can tell he's been around."

I hesitate.

"How?" I ask.

She looks at me.

"Someone's been taking food from the refrigerator."

"Adam?"

She nods.

"I see him sometimes," she says. "I saw him last night. I saw him walking through the backyard."

I look at her to try and determine if something's wrong with her.

"I try to keep watch for him. I sit at the back window. It seems like he only comes out at night but I sometimes watch for him during the day."

"Where do you think he's staying?" I ask.

She shrugs.

"I don't know."

21.

I looked for Adam the next day. I didn't see him in the hall-way or at his locker and I didn't see him outside in the pack of kids flooding out the front doors of the school. I was ready to give up when I spotted Adam walking across the parking lot of the apartment complex next to the school. He had skipped going to his locker and had taken the side exit to avoid another confrontation. He was walking with his head down and his back to the school and his backpack had been replaced with a plastic grocery bag which he carried in his hand.

Adam crossed the street and made his way across the park. I jogged to catch up with him. He made a quick defensive turn as he heard me approaching from behind.

"What's up?" I asked, smiling.

He relaxed.

"Hi," he said.

I hadn't planned on what to say to him. I had only known that I was going to make an effort to be nice to him. We wound up walking across the park in silence. Adam felt no pressure to fill dead air. I tried to think of something to say. I had never been punched and I wanted to ask him what it was like but that didn't seem appropriate.

"Why did you go in that house yesterday?" I finally asked.

Adam looked at me as if the answer was obvious.

"To get away from Pat."

"Right," I said.

"A good way to get rid of a person is to go somewhere that they won't go."

"Interesting," I said. I wondered if maybe he learned that from his older brother. Maybe Adam knew about his brother going into the woods.

I waited for him to say more but he didn't.

"What was it like inside the house?" I asked.

He looked at the ground and was quiet for a moment.

"It was nice," he said. "There was a giant curling staircase in the front hallway."

"What did you do when you went inside?"

Adam looked at me and blinked. He had big eyes with dark rings underneath them. He would grow into them as he got older.

"Well, I thought I heard someone walking around upstairs so I hurried deeper into the house to look for the back door so I could get out of there. I walked past an enormous living room and there was a woman in there wiping down a picture frame with a rag."

"Did she see you?" I asked.

"No," he said, shaking his head. "Her back was to me. I walked further back into a room with a bunch of couches and skylights and windows. There was a sliding glass door that led out into the backyard. I slid it open and walked out onto the cement deck."

Adam was staring intently in front of him as he walked. He could see the scene he described. I think Adam had a pretty good imagination.

"I was going to run off into the backyard but there was a pool and it just looked really nice glimmering there in the sun. I stopped and looked at it for a moment. I thought about jumping in to refresh myself and get some of the blood and dirt off me. Then I heard the porch door sliding open behind me. I turned around and saw that it was the woman who was in the living room. She was standing at the porch door."

"What did she say?" I asked.

"She asked me what I was doing but she didn't seem mad. I guess I looked pretty funny standing there without a shirt on and blood smeared on my face. I told her I wasn't doing anything and then I said sorry and I ran into the backyard and pushed my way through the bushes. The bushes scraped my stomach."

He lifted up his shirt to show me a long pink scratch across his ribs.

"What did you do then?" I asked.

"I found my way home."

I was intrigued by Adam's description. The odd specifics convinced me of its validity.

"Wow," I said.

He nodded his head. I tried to think of something else to say.

"I hear Pat wants to fight me again," said Adam.

"Maybe," I said. "No one likes Pat. Maybe you should just fight him. You might win."

"I don't fight people," he said.

We approached a corner.

"I guess I'll turn here," I said.

"Hey, do you like to play games?" asked Adam.

It was a strange question.

"Sure," I said, trying to be friendly.

"I have an idea for a game. It's called 'Town.' We basically play people in the neighborhood. We have money and a job. It's like a real town but we play in one of our basements. We could play in my basement. We would try to make it as real as possible. Like a real town. We'd have taxes, and a police station, and food."

Adam went quiet. He looked at me.

"Do you think you'd play a game like that?" he asked.

"Yeah, I said. "That sounds like fun." Though the idea seemed vague and somehow unsettling.

"Cool," he said. "We should do it soon."

22.

I go out to the back porch to have a cigarette. It's windy and I have to hold my hand up to my face to get my cigarette lit. I look up into the ash tree, at the wind blowing the leaves. I look further out into the yard at the apple tree. Behind the tree is the house of the people who I've never met. I can see the windows of their house lit up. There's a powerful gust of wind and I hear a thump as an apple drops from the apple tree. I look closely at the darkness; I'm trying to see Adam back there. Walking through yards.

I go inside and shut the door behind me. I walk into the kitchen. Dennis and Pam are watching a movie in the neighboring room. I consider joining them but I don't want to. My mind is still on Adam. I think about what he said. The best way to get away from someone is to go somewhere that they won't go.

I decide to go for a walk. I have to tug hard on the front door; there's suction from the wind. Dirt is blowing around as I move out onto the front steps. A speck of grit gets in my eye. I blink several times and squeeze my eyes shut. Tears leak out. The dirt clears and the irritation fades. When I look up, I think I see someone across the street running through the streetlight but when my eyes stop watering, I see that it's just shadow of a tree branch blowing in front of the streetlight.

I walk down the street towards the park. My hands are in my pockets. I'm thinking through Adam's disappearance.

I stop on the street corner. I look across the street and see a raccoon waddle across a lawn and swing itself down into a sewage grate.

I cross the street and walk towards the park. I look at the tops of the trees blowing in the wind. The treetops are dark against the sky and seem to move in slow motion. I stop at the edge of the woods. I can barely see into them.

I walk along the edge of the woods to where there's an overgrown trail entrance. I push the branches aside and duck my head. I clear the branches and continue down the dirt path. I stop when I'm at the center of the woods. I stand and listen. The sound of the wind in the trees is loud above me.

I step off the path. My eyes have adjusted to the darkness but it's still difficult to see. I step carefully through the underbrush and wind my way through the trees. I scan the forest for movement. I hear occasional scurrying sounds but when I look towards them I don't see anything.

I come out of the woods into the moonlight. Ahead of me are the railroad tracks beyond which the forest continues. The rocks shift under my feet as I walk up the tracks. I step onto the metal rail and down onto the wooden tie. I look far down the tracks and see cars crossing over Maple Road. Beyond the railroad crossing is the high school football stadium which is dark for the summer.

I continue down the other side of the tracks and back into the woods. The distant sound of cars grows louder as I walk through the trees. I continue to look for movement but see none.

I get tired of searching and stop to have another smoke. I pluck a cigarette out of the pack. I light the cigarette, tilt my head back, and look up into the trees. I see something moving amongst the branches. A dark shape. I watch and see it move again. I take a step to the side to try and make it out but I can't. I take out my lighter and raise it above my head. I try lighting it but the wind is too strong. I hold up my other hand and cup it around the lighter. I spark several times and the lighter ignites. The light reflects off a pair of eyes in the tree. The eyes are silver and close to one another. A raccoon looks down at me; a bandit mask around its small silver eyes.

I continue through the forest and the sound of Maple Street grows louder. I can see the lights of the road up ahead of me. I walk towards the lights and come out of the trees into a field. I look around me and see the gazebo where Lindsay and I have stretched before going for a run. The street is busy with traffic, cars pass up and down the street.

I look over at the restaurants and bars along Maple. Aurelio's restaurant is lit up. There are people eating dinner out on the porch. Across from the restaurant is a bar; there's a green awning in front of it. Underneath the awning, men and women drunkenly talk to one another. I see one woman leaning on another woman. She's yelling at a man about something but, even from this distance, I can tell that the yelling is a type of flirtation.

I hurry across the street and continue into the woods on the other side. No one seems to see me. This part of the forest is easy. There's a mulch trail that I walk down. To my left is a prairie garden. The grass is taller than me. I wonder if perhaps Adam would be hiding in there but that seems dangerous. Too tall, too many hidden creatures in the grass. I look at the grass. The wind makes it roll like waves on water.

The path eventually slopes down to the creek. A thick stretch of prairie grass and weeds runs along the water. I push my way through the prairie grass. I stop at the creek and look at the muddy brown water streaming past. The stench of the water is strong. It smells foul and polluted. An image comes back to me that I saw in a local history book of the creek from the twenties. Kids were swimming in it. Maybe it was still polluted back then, too. Maybe they just didn't know any better.

The soles of my shoes make sucking sounds on the mud

as I walk along the bank. The wind blows so strongly at times that I have to put out my arms out to keep my balance. I pass under a walking bridge and look up at the dark underside of it. I imagine something hiding up there in the rusty metal.

Past the bridge, I stop and look off into the forest that runs along the creek. The trees are dense. Over the sound of the wind, I can hear voices of teenagers calling out to one another and laughing. Adam can't be in there. If he were in those woods, he'd be found.

I turn and look across the creek. I'm looking at a patch of land. I've seen this place before. This is where John and I stopped when we were cleaning out the woods. A small urban island surrounded on three sides by a tall chainlink fence, the highway, and the creek. I remember what John said about that place. That's where people would go to fuck. Then I remember what Adam said. A good way to get away from people is to go somewhere that they won't go.

I look at the creek. It's wide but it seems to be shallow along the sides. I try to estimate about how far it is from one shallow side of the creek to the other. Maybe about ten feet. I think back to high school when I used to do long jump. I remember clearing twelve feet. I don't think about it. I walk back into the prairie, pushing the grass away from me, clearing a path. I stand at the back of the weeds and crouch down. I look at the far side of the creek. I breath in deep and take off in a sprint. I speed forward, step into the water, and launch off. I see the water passing under me in my periphery. My muscle memory comes back. I kick my legs ahead of me like I used to do. I come down in the shallow end of the other side of the creek. Water splashes up unto me as I feel the solidness of the ground under my feet. I grunt and stumble forward up onto the bank.

"Holy shit," I mutter to myself. I look at my feet. My shoes and ankles are wet and muddy but nothing else. It's unbelievable. I stand at the bank for a moment, appreciating the exhilaration of having jumped over a creek.

I turn towards the trees. The patch of forest is on an incline. A small hill crowded with trees. I walk up the bank towards the dense woods. The moonlight cuts out as I step into them. I can hear the expressway over the other side of the hill. I stop and look around me. It occurs to me to say something, to say Adam's name but I don't. It seems silly.

As I think this, there's a sudden movement off to my left and something goes running. I see a person sprinting up the hill. I squint but can't make them out before they're lost in the darkness. Maybe it's two people, I can't tell. I force myself to run up the hill. As I run, my foot slips on something that feels like fabric, maybe a blanket. My other foot kicks something and it makes a clattering sound.

I push my way up the hill and around the trees. I crest the hill and look down. It's much brighter over here. An eerie flat light from the highway covers the trees on this side of the hill. There's a chain link fence about halfway down the hill that separates the highway with it's zipping cars from the forest. Past the fence, it's all grass.

I look around me at the trees. They cast long dark shadows. They look like people. My eyes move slowly across them.

"Adam," I say. "Is that you?"

My eyes stop at a tree near the edge of the fence. I can see the side of a person behind the tree.

"Adam?" I ask again. "Are you alright?"

I wonder whether it's him. I walk slowly along the side of the tree and more of the person becomes visible. In the faint light from the highway, I can see the side of his face and the top of his head. I can see his receding hairline. He's not looking at me. He's looking away but he seems aware that I'm looking at him.

I look at him for a moment to see if he'll look at me but he doesn't. He just keeps looking away off to the side. I wait long enough to know that he knows I see him and he's aware that

I'm there.

"It's Vince Ford," I say. "The one who found you next to the quarry."

He looks off into the distance.

"Do you need anything?"

I wait to see for a response.

"No thanks," he finally says. "I'm fine."

"You're sure you're okay?" I ask.

"Yes," he says.

I stand there for a moment and listen to the hum of the highway. I turn and walk back towards the creek.

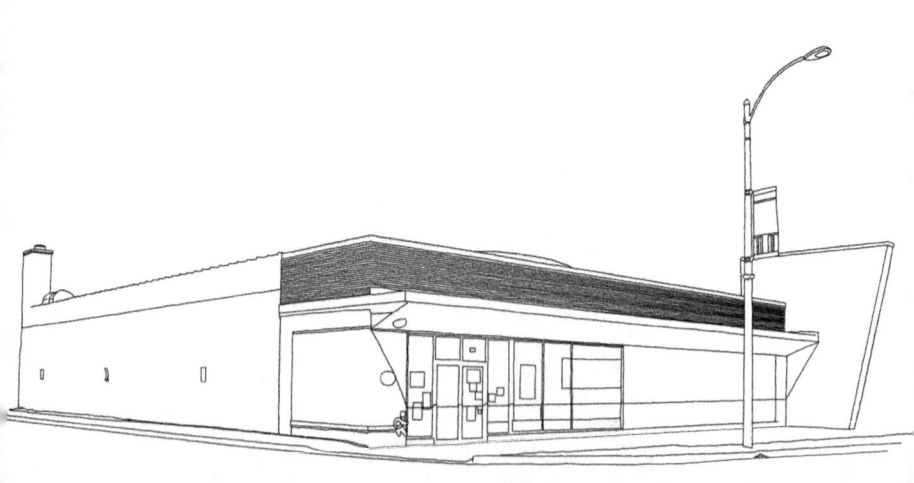

23.

My dad says he's going to run errands and I ask if I can come with him. Dennis and Pam decide to come as well. In the car, I look out the window at the passing houses and I think about Adam. The night before seems like a strange dream.

Pam gets a call as we're walking into the hardware store. She looks at Dennis. Her eyes are wide and excited.

"I think it's about the fellowship," she says.

She answers the phone and walks down the sidewalk.

"I'll hang out here," says Dennis.

My dad and I go in. My dad walks into the store looking for the the items on his list while I wander around. I look around at the old men in red vests with nametags on them. I look at the cashier. He's ringing up a woman. He's an old man with thick bifocals and a trucker's hat. He looks familiar and I try to place him.

It takes a moment but it comes to me. It's Samuel, John's co-worker from the cemetery. The one who we watched get harassed in the video. He's older now. His hairline has receded. His hair is more yellow than white. His eyes are watery and pink.

Samuel swipes the woman's card and hands it back to her.

"Have a good day," he says and I hear his voice for the first time. It's high-pitched. I almost laugh when I hear it. It sounds like the voice of a cartoon character. No wonder he was made fun of by the guys at the cemetery. I try to imagine his life from beginning to end while I wait for my dad.

When we go outside Pam is still on her phone. She's walking back and forth next to the police station. She has one finger in her opposite ear so she can hear better. She has a smile on her face.

We stop next to Dennis.

"I think she got the fellowship," he says, watching her pace. I look at Dennis as he watches her. I see pride and infatuation in his eyes.

"Great," says my dad.

"She's going to save the world," I say.

"Yeah," says Dennis and I can see in his eyes that he thinks it's true.

Acknowledgments

A special thanks to Vedran Vujasinovic for providing feedback throughout the writing process. Thank you to Gail Siegel for providing an insightful close read. Thanks to Lisa Yarte for your thoughts on the covers. Thanks to all of the kind people at R018 and R284 for your support and kindness. Thanks to Charlie Reibsamen and Brian Haag for being great roommates and great people. Thanks to Tommy Baldwin for the encouragement. Thank you to my family for your continual support.

This book and the corresponding movie only exist because of the generosity of a wonderful group of people. A big thank you to all of the following Kickstarter contributors:

Aaron Glenn	Bethany Geraghty	Chaitan Dabhade
Adam Boucher	Betty Lee Kim	Chandra Hammond
Adam Hinrichs	Betty Sublette	Charles Laliberte
Adrian Parrish	Bob Liu	Charlie Reibsamen
Alex Loomer	Bonnie Kaplan	Chris Louis
Alicia Carney	Brendan Donaldson	Christine Bunuan
Allison Corn	Brendan Dowling	Christine Huck
Andrew Bendelow	Brendon Culhane	Christine McKenna
Andrew Hillard	Brett Ingle	Eartheart
Andrew MacRae	Brian A Tilden	Christopher Moran
Andrew Stasiulis	Brian George	Christopher Selfridge
Andrew Stoll	Brian Kidd	Christy Wirig
Andy Martin	Brian Sebby	Claire Jennings
Angelo Campos	Brian Selvaggio	Claudia Burgener
Angelos Goudis	Brian Urbanik	Courtney B Collins
Anisa Dema	Bryan Keithley	Courtney Herrmann
Annie Niehoff	Caleb Dietz	Courtney LeStarge
Anthony Ac Chandler	Calvin Reeder	Cynthia Jones
Aretta Swanson	Candace Snapp	Dan Grainge
Ashley Suski	Carly Statz	Dan Isaacson
Ashlyn Tessema	Carol Kostelny	Dan McDonald
Bernadette Haberna	Carol Wilson	Dan Osten
Dos	Carolina Silva	Daniel Cady

Daniel DiFranco
Daniel Ibrahim
Danielle Swanson
Danny Craig
Darlene Kirschbaum
David Auburn
David Henderson
David Scott Crawford
David Ward
Dawn Feit
Denis Vujasinovic
Denise McDade
Derek Bukiema
Devin Ruddy
Diane Eidelman
Dominic Bruno
Dustin Deal
Dylan Jeffery
Edward Todd
Elena Costales
Elizabeth
Ellen Christensen
Emily Schappler
Erik Johnson
Erik Stonikas
Erin Tinnon
Fred Ciba
Fred Fang
Garrison Burk
Gary Lawrence
George Manisco
Georgy Das
Gina Peshek
Gordon Magill
Greg McLaughlin
GrownUp KidStuff
Gwendolyn Infusino
Heather
Heather Kuhl

Heidi Dollinger
Honna George
Irene Bowen
Irvana Vujasinovic
Jack Zimmerman
Jackie Ni
Jahan Rodriguez
James Kline
James Larkin
James O'Sullivan
Jamie Tiplitsky
Jan Head
Jane Connors
Jane Nolan Heffernan
Jason Brusa
Jason Flamm
Jason Lewis
Jason Snelson
Jay Gammill
Jayne Williams
Jaysen Cryer
Jeff Angarola
Jeff Ash
Jeff Bengtson
Jeff Martin
Jeff Wood
Jeffrey Linton
Jeffrey Norris
Jenna Heffernan
Jennifer Hobbs
Jennifer Phillips
Jennifer Smith
Jeremiah Jordan
Jeremy O'Sullivan
Jeremy Tregler
Jesse Kriske
Jesse Lawson
Jessica Hackner
Jim Connors

Joe Jansen
Joel Hatstat
Joel Spezeski
John Frantz
John Langen
John Paulett
John Randle
John Reibsamen
Jon Fronza
Jon Jones
Jonathan Coleman
Joni Lindemer
Joseph Dicianni
Joshua Bretl
Joyce Delisi
Judith O'Sullivan
Judy Skwiertz Vogt
Judy Thrall
Julia Jane Sparkman
Julie Maxwell
Justin T. Parsons
Karen Kusmierz
Karen Pfeifer
Karen Todd
Kari Marcum
Kat Rybarski
Kate Seiwert
Katelyn Beaty
Kathleen Murphy Adams
Kathy Goss
Katie Amundsen
Katie Enright
Katie Todd Nussbaum
Katie Triska Wiemer
Katy Colloton
Kay & Bud Selfridge
Kelley Westwood
Ken Kuchar

Kevin Devine
Kevin McKernan
Kieran Lee Farr
Kimberly Bolich
Kris Davidson
Kristin Balon
Lance Russ
Laura Hillard
Laura Milkert
Laura Zinger
Lauren Garcia
Lil BUB
Lily Reed
Lisa Yarte
Liz Fagan
Loren R. Tieman
Lya Guerra
Lydia Bright
Lynn Montei
Mackie Berman
Marcia Peters
Marian Nealon
Marianne Angarola
Marisa Weisman
Mark Rivera
Martin Nelan
Martyn Jones
Mary Filice
Mary Kriske
Maryellen Rafalski
Matt Ahrens
Mazher Abbas
Megan Feit
Megan Roberts
Melissa McKenzie
Melissa Zepeda
Michael Bradt
Michael Olsen
Mike Bridavsky

Mike O'Shea
Molly Meinbresse
Molly Russell
Morgan Terrill
Nancy Nega
Nancy Price
Natasha Kohli
Nate Parkes
Nathan Dietz
Nels Bangerter
Nicholas Fasolt
Nicole Grimes
Nikko Mazzone
Noah Stroehle
Paddy Cassidy
Patricia Arnoldt
Patrick Callaghan
Patrick Knudsen
Patrick Reilley
Patt Cheney
Paul Metzger
Paul T. Anderson
Paula Caballero
Pauline Eveillard
Payal Khandhar
Peter Martin
Peter Podgursky
Rachel Deckert
Rachel Hamblen
Rachel Hood
Randall Hoole
Randall Louis Cooper
Rexie M. Deato
Reza Mirzaie
Rick Castaneda
Rick Todd
Rob Madden
Ron Nicholas
Rosemary Cooke

Windsor
Roz Long
Ryan Anderson
Ryan Bales
Ryan Durkin
Ryan Gilleran
Saad Hussain
Sandra Yencho
Sara Delcourt
Sarah Hill
Sasha Cuttler
Scott Keiler
Scott Klapperich
Scott Martin
Scottie Long Productions, Inc.
Sean Williams
Seth T. Hahne
Soraya Aghai
Stacy Bridavsky
Stephanie Howes
Stephen Osters
Stephen Scott
Stephen Wilcox
Steve Greenspon
Steve Martins
Steve Springmeyer
Steve Waste
Susan Thiel
Susan Todd-Bedell
Suzanne Martin
Suzanne Martin
T M
Taylor Overstreet
Terra Cooney
Terrence Madden
The Improv Shop
The Martin-Venema Family

The Selfridge Family
Themi Psarras
Theresa Martin
Theresa Petru
Therese golden
Thom Murray
Thomaie Hilaris
Thomas Hams
Tim Hillegonds
Tim Soszko
Tim Walsh
Tina Tews
Todd Jones
Tommy Baldwin
Tracy Madden
Tricia Speziale
Val Anthony Fox
Vedran Vujasinovic
Ward Roberts
Westside Improv
Whitney Peterson
Zack Mast

www.CookeConcrete.com